Rachel Seiffert's first novel, *The D[...]*
Man Booker Prize and was mad[...]
was named as one of *Granta's* [...]
2003, and in 2011 she receive[...]
American Academy of Arts an[...]
of short stories, received an av[...] r
second novel, *Afterwards* and [...] e
longlisted for the Orange/Ba[...] [...]. Her books have been
published in eighteen languages. Rachel Seiffert lives in London
with her family.

'Seiffert's prose is not showy, but graceful and precise. The misery
of the dank streets is relieved by flashes of light and humanity'
The Economist

'A fine novel that locates small, flickering lights of hope in an
otherwise desolate landscape'   Nick Rennison, *Sunday Times*

'Rachel Seiffert writes short, fast narratives about the big historical
events that have shaped our time'   John Sutherland, *The Times*

'Rachel Seiffert's new novel *A Boy in Winter* stretches over only
three days, through which you encounter all the emotions of the
time, horror and instinct for survival, family loyalty, and above all
perhaps, bravery'   James Naughtie, BBC World TV

'Spare, elegant and devastating'   *Psychologies*

'Seiffert's writing is spare and atmospheric, perfectly paced to
achieve the maximum effect of stillness yielding to panic, order
giving way to violent disorder and, eventually, winter turning into
spring'   *Times Literary Supplement*

A BOY IN WINTER

RACHEL SEIFFERT

virago

VIRAGO

First published in Great Britain in 2017 by Virago Press
This paperback edition published in 2018 by Virago Press

3 5 7 9 10 8 6 4 2

A CIP catalogue record for this book
is available from the British Library.

ISBN 978-1-84408-999-4

Typeset in Garamond by M Rules
Printed and bound in Great Britain by
Clays Ltd, St Ives plc

Papers used by Virago are from well-managed forests
and other responsible sources.

Virago Press
An imprint of
Little, Brown Book Group
Carmelite House
50 Victoria Embankment
London EC4Y 0DZ

An Hachette UK Company
www.hachette.co.uk

www.virago.co.uk

For Edie

He said the wicked know that if the evil they do is of sufficient horror men will not speak against it. That men have only stomach for small evils and only these will they oppose.

Cormac McCarthy, The Crossing

I have never felt equal to the business.

Viktor Klemperer, To the Bitter End

A BOY
IN WINTER

Ukraine, November 1941

1

He is out and running in the first grey of morning.

Ducked and noiseless, hurrying through the fog drifts with his brother just behind him; feeling the tug of his small fingers twisted in a fistful of his jerkin, crossing the cobbles of the empty town streets, just as day is breaking.

Already they have made it past the railway station, the distillery and the cooper's yard, and then all along the silent length of the market street. Unseen, unheard – at least as yet.

When they reach the old church at the corner, the boy stops, pulling his young brother close, pressing both of them to the stone walls and listening a moment.

He hears nothing and no one; no sounds of movement. The boy's darting eyes see no lamplight behind the curtains, only shutters drawn across the windows. They have been flitting from street to street and hiding, but the boy sees no place here they can slip inside. The fog hangs damp between the houses, and along the winding street before him, shrouding the low roofs and the lane mouths, the huddle of timbered house fronts. At least there is no one here yet to find them.

Soon, he thinks. *It will come soon now.* Didn't the schoolmaster say so?

His brother tugs at his fingers, holding up his arms to be lifted, and the boy pulls him onto his back to carry him; still cautious and casting looks about himself, but picking up his pace too. They left the house in darkness, only now the low clouds are paling, and he feels the day and its dangers drawing nearer.

He feels his brother shivering too, clutched to his shoulders, the short night's bed-warmth long out of him. But it is better they do this. Better they make for the old schoolmaster's lodgings. They still have more than half the town to cross, but even so: the boy thinks the old schoolmaster will know – who they can turn to, or the best place to lie low.

Then comes the flare of headlamps, a sudden glare in the fog beyond them; the crunch of tyres, of heavy vehicles halting on flagstones.

His brother grips him, small fists tight and fearful, and then already the boy is turning, already he is running, making for the shelter of one of the town's many alleyways – even before he hears the rumbling of all the many vehicles following.

Otto Pohl wakes to the noise of a door slam. One truck door, then another, below his boarding-house window: loud reports echoing across the town square beyond his half-drawn curtains.

He must have left them half drawn last night, too weary

and chilled to notice. Still fogged with sleep, for a short time all Pohl can see is the leaded squares above his bedpost, framing the town-hall clock and schoolhouse, squat in the autumn mist; this squat and damp place he's been posted.

'*Zeigt euch!*'

'*Pokazhit'sya!*'

Is it German? Pohl thinks he hears Ukrainian shouted. But his foremen and workers are all quartered well beyond here, out in open country, and it is too early to be waking, surely. The grey outside is a before-dawn kind, and he has not slept well since he arrived here; Pohl has not been able, and he needs to rest. There is that shouting again.

'*Mach schon!*'

Shrill and coarse. *Some fool out there is playing at soldiers.* Pohl pulls the blankets higher around his shoulders: he will pay them no regard. *Who can have any regard for what soldiers do? For armies?* he asks his Dorle. Although she is miles from here.

His wife is far away in Münster, but Pohl talks to her most mornings. Silently, inwardly, he turns his thoughts homewards, seeking comfort. Thinking of the sound of her, somewhere in the house beyond him; of rising to find her buttoning her coat at the hallway mirror, tucking her curls under the firm hold of her hat brim, then pulling out just enough of them as the bells sound the first service. Or waiting in the pews with their small daughter while she takes communion, before walking home again, arm in arm through the Sunday *Altstadt* quiet.

But now more trucks are arriving, loud below his window. And although Pohl has his covers pulled against them, he is awake. Thoughts of home can't block them out. Or that shouting either.

'*Ihr sollt euch zeigen!*'

Too loud to ignore, it has Pohl confounded; it has him disordered, sitting up, pulling on his shirt. He can't find his glasses. He has to get up to feel for them: on the desk at his bedside, in his engineering corps trousers hanging on the chair back; and all the while it continues, this bellowing and ordering, this ungodly noise at this ungodly hour of the morning.

Pohl hears dull thuds falling as he fumbles down the unlit stairwell. Are they hammer blows? Discharges? He can only half make them out through the thick boarding-house walls as he reaches the foot of the staircase, searching his tunic pockets, still looking for his glasses.

The stoves are all dark, and there is no one in the kitchen. Up even before the housemaid, Pohl has the out-of-sorts feeling this day has started far too early; it has started all wrong somehow.

Stooping at the window beside the low front entrance, he finds his glasses, finally, and hooks them over his ears, peering across to the town hall, looking for the clock, sure it has missed its hourly strike – or is he the one who has missed it?

What he sees out there brings him up short.

Soldiers. On the town square. Field-grey uniforms: *Wehrmacht* in the fog.

It is not the first time he's seen field grey here. Although he's told Dorle the territory is secure now. *It has been secured for rebuilding; they are done with their* Blitzkrieg, *I can promise you this much.*

Pohl is careful with his words to her; in his weekly letters, of course, because – the times being what they are – heaven knows who might read them; but also in his daily mumbled thoughts and reports, because Pohl feels Dorle deserves this care – she would hate so much of what he sees here.

The SS convoys, for one thing.

Here in such numbers, they rake through the countryside. There were SS jeeps only the day before yesterday, passing in a dark line along the horizon beyond Pohl's roadworks.

His foreman pointed them out.

'Sir.'

A man of few words, he tilted his chin in the convoy's direction, and then they both raised their heads from Pohl's drawings, pausing at their work to squint at the speeding vehicles while the labourers toiled on behind them. The jeeps were too far to hear against the pickaxe blows and the prevailing wind, but they were swift, that much was certain, seen against the slow crawl of their building progress.

Pohl had his fingers gripped to the road plans, the wind tugging at his paper version of the highway they were already behind on, but he stood and watched the convoy instead of returning to the task before him. Because close behind the SS jeeps came another unit: Order Police first, sent from Germany, and then so many *Wehrmacht* vehicles, such a long line of them. One jeep, one truck after another. Enough soldiers to have Pohl counting, to have Pohl mistrustful. Why so many soldiers behind the lines?

Now here he is at the window. Rooted, caught by the figures gathering on the town square: it is the same mix of grey and black uniforms in front of the schoolhouse. Has the same convoy come to the town?

Such a crowd of them; it seems there are always more, and Pohl can't understand all their calling. Some is German, some just unintelligible, and he doesn't like their urgency, or the way they are always moving: always more groups of them forming, as though readying for something. Still he has to keep watching because in amongst the shouting come new sounds: not just hammering but cracking too now, and splintering. And then Pohl hears rather than sees the school-house door kicked open.

The noise of this jars him.

He sees lights inside the school, and they are moving. Electric torches; Pohl follows their progress as they pass the windows. The soldiers pass along the ground floor first, then up the back stairs – so they are searching the place. More: it sounds as though they are hurling things; school desks and school chairs.

A pane is struck, upstairs, a window on the upper floor, the glass bursting outwards, then scattering across the flagstones.

Are they turning the place over?

Pohl hears shouting – harsh, from inside – and then the soldiers spill out again. Glass shards grinding underfoot, torch beams swinging this way and that, they surge back onto the town square – such a mass of them – while he can only stand and watch, still with the feeling that he is barely keeping up, not understanding nearly enough.

And then an old man and an even older woman are bundled out of the doorway and onto the paving.

Grey and stooped, his schoolmaster's frock coat torn across the shoulders, the old man puts an arm up, pleading. It is a shielding arm above the older woman's frame, Pohl can see this.

Her face, pale in the torch beams, is turned upward in confusion, to the booted figures who have come to stand over them.

'*Aufstehen!*'

They are ordered to stand.

'*Mach schon!*'

They are ordered to run.

They are herded; they are *herded* – Pohl can find no other word for it. Three soldiers behind them, even more ahead, the two old people are run down the cobbled street.

'*Lauf, Dreckjude!*'

The schoolmaster hears boots on flagstones, ahead and behind him; slammed doors, slammed windows, as he is chased through the grey lanes beyond the town hall.

'*Raus! Aus den Häusern!*'

Stumbling in the half-light and confusion, he reaches for his mother amid the fog and the calling.

'*Alle Juden! Alle Juden draussen.*'

So close to his mother tongue, his mother's Yiddish tones, the old teacher can understand the orders, even before they are repeated in Ukrainian. 'All Jews, outside!' Even as he struggles to keep pace with the SS men who bellow them.

'All Jews! *All* of you!'

'Now, we say!'

There are a dozen SS around him – hounding him, hounding his mother – and there are still others beyond them: they seem to fill the small town's streets and alleyways. So many more than he thought, the schoolmaster had not anticipated even nearly so large a force. But now he is run past whole packs of soldiers, of policemen crowded at the corners, standing wide-legged at the house doors and pounding.

If he had only known this.

That soldiers would come hauling people out of their houses.

That police would come looking in such numbers. For any who refused to comply with the instruction.

'Juden, zeigt euch!'

'Show yourselves!'

'All Jews are to show themselves.'

They were to be at the brickworks at six. One suitcase of belongings, winter clothing, food for three days' travel; *make ready for your resettlement.* But the schoolmaster had decided: he was too long in the tooth to be given such orders, and his mother too frail for travelling anywhere.

Her old cheeks wrinkled like winter apples, old eyes searching his, 'But we are not allowed,' she'd told him, as he hushed her, ushering her through the schoolhouse doorway yesterday evening. 'You are not allowed in here, *meyn yingle.'*

There are so many things forbidden them since the Germans came, and she is frail now, in mind as well as limb, it was too hard for her to understand why they should lie low there, in the disused classrooms; it was all too convoluted – and too dispiriting – to explain to her.

But the schoolmaster had thought they only need lie low for a day or two. So he'd urged his mother gently up the wooden stairway, cracking and groaning under their combined weight, all the while thinking how he'd taught the town officials who issued this German order. Men he'd thought were decent, but who had offered their services to the new authorities, hot-foot, so soon after the invasion. *Such opportunists. What has happened to their scruples?* Two generations, three generations; for three decades, almost, he'd taught this town's children. Reading and writing, respect for their elders. Wrong from right, too. *Have they retained nothing?*

These thoughts consumed him last night, and now he could curse himself for thinking them. Holding tight to his mother to keep her from stumbling, the master berates himself for wasting time. All those hours he spent resenting, he should have been thinking on the morning; on what the SS might do when he wasn't at the brickworks as ordered, and when they found his house deserted.

'*Scheissjuden!*'

Because now they are driven past one house front after another where the soldiers swarm, furious; all the front doors flung wide, half the windows also.

'*Leer!*'

The SS shout from the upper floors, disgusted at finding them empty.

'*Scheissjuden! Ich sag's dir!*'

The policemen tear down the curtains, they tip the linen chests out onto the paving, and the schoolmaster is pressed onwards over all the scattered housewares, thinking those people must have been given warning. He was warned too, after all – and he knows now he should have heeded it.

One of his former pupils – one of those opportunists – came to the house after the order was issued. Under cover of darkness, without his chains of office.

'Wise to do as they ask.' That was his best advice. He

stood between the narrow walls of the old master's stairwell, this provincial official who'd been one of his most diligent students, and he whispered: 'You should comply. Or make yourselves scarce, you and your mother there. I am sorry. I am sorry to tell you this.'

But the schoolmaster hadn't wanted to hear those apologies. And his pride wouldn't let him run from the Germans.

Now the soldiers turn on them. They turn and shout and shove at him, rough with their fists and elbows, pushing hard into his mother to stop the two of them running, and the schoolmaster has to throw his arms out to take hold of her, to stop them hurting her, as they are herded through a doorway.

They are run down a dark passageway – too dark to see the way ahead – and he keeps a firm grip of his mother's arm, reaching out with his other palm, pressing it to the wall they are pushed along, trying to hold himself upright. The floor below is brick and damp and worn away, and he has to press hard to keep both of them from falling; the old teacher struggles to keep pace with the soldiers, and all the while he tries to place himself: they have been chased through half the town's streets and he has not been able to follow where the soldiers have taken them.

But then the soldiers fall abruptly away from them.

The noise of their shouting recedes, the passage widens and clears, and he can slow again; he can look around himself.

There are high brick walls on either side, and high works doorways: they've been brought to the old brick factory.

They have been brought here anyway.

The order was to be here at six. It can't be much later

now, the schoolmaster thinks, as they slow to a halt in the passageway, and he grapples with his thoughts again. He has kept hold of his mother's arm, so thin inside its sleeve, and he feels how she leans into him, bird-boned and fearful. He had wanted to spare her this. He had wanted to spare her, but here they are anyway – and surely this is worse, this harrying from the soldiers.

The ones who ran them here have fallen behind them and, glancing back, still apprehensive, the schoolmaster sees they are gathering at the entrance to the passageway. Bent over, leaning at the door frame, they are catching their breath, and others are joining them out on the street beyond the doorway; did they chase down more of the townsfolk? Did more hide like him? The schoolmaster hopes – briefly – that more are still hiding. And that they hid well enough for the Germans not to find them.

'Forwards! Get moving.'

The schoolmaster does as he is told as new shouts come from ahead of them, this time all in Ukrainian.

'Get a move on.'

Three policemen stand, coshes raised, at the passageway's farthest end, and the old teacher moves his hands swiftly to his mother's shoulders. He sees grey light leaking through the door there: dawn has come, and he wants this harrying to be over.

The door is pushed open.

He sees a room full of faces. Full of shoulders and coats, and hats and suitcases. But it is mostly the faces the school-master takes in: pale and cowed, bewildered, they turn to the door and the latest to join them.

There are a hundred in there. *More.* Perhaps it is nearer two, or even three: it is a press of people.

The schoolmaster sees the small factory floor has been pressed full. Not just of townsfolk; *it can't be.* It must be Jews from all over the district. *Who knew we were so many?* This throng of faces comes as a surprise to him, a sudden comfort, even. But then a cosh is pressed between his shoulder blades.

The master is shoved into this crowd, his mother after him, so the nearest must jostle and shift to make room for them. Shoulders part, arms and backs, but there are too many in here already, there is no more room to be had, and the shove the old man got was too hard.

He staggers forward, losing his footing. Lurching now, he lets go of his mother, for fear of her falling also.

'Oh!'

Then a hand comes out and grasps him.

'Schoolmaster!'

It comes from among the backs and elbows, and the old teacher reaches for his helper; he reaches in gratitude.

Only for a cosh to fall behind him.

A blow to the head that fells him.

2

Pohl drives too fast, and a different route than his usual, sending the car lurching across the town bridge to leave the place swiftly, his stomach tight with the shock and the shame of it – that his countrymen do this; that he is here to see it happening.

The town spires recede first, in the fog in the rear-view mirror, then the factory chimney, and still he jolts further along the cart tracks into open country, putting the miles behind him. Pohl can't see far through the lifting mist, but even when he reaches the line of the roadworks, he still drives onwards, crossing the rubble thoroughfare his labourers have laid so far, rather than skirting along it as he usually would. On any other day, he might drive from labour gang to labour gang on his inspection rounds, or head for his office at the encampment, but Pohl has no thoughts of work this morning, just of putting distance between himself and the soldiers.

He has seen far too much of what they do – even just on the journey to take up this posting.

They crawled across this landscape to get here, Pohl and his small advance troop of workers. It took days of driving in convoy across Germany and Poland, and then the vast and rolling grassland beyond the Ukrainian border. Through the heat-haze and downpours of the August thunderstorms; on the heels of the invasion; over the tank ruts and across the craters.

Pohl took these in with dismay: all the blast-holes and gouges left in the *Wehrmacht*'s wake, in the path of the Soviets' retreat. The further east, the worse it got: after they crossed the river Bug, the roadside ditches were filled to overflowing, not just with floodwater but with slaughtered Red Army horses, Red Army corpses. Pohl had steeled himself for damage, even for carnage, but not on this scale; and he was unprepared, also, for how long it was simply left in place, to bloat and to decay. It seemed to him a desecration.

He wrote to Dorle: *There is nothing left of some places, just wreckage.* Barns had been mortared, left blackened and roofless; where once had been farmsteads and grain-stores, outbuildings, only the gable-ends were left standing, charred and listing, their burned-out shells visible for miles across the wide plains.

He saw looted churches, empty and open to the elements, their windows and doorways broken. Entire towns had been ransacked – *such barbarity* – crossroads and bridges blasted, wooden pylons left in splinters, cables in shreds and tangles.

In whole days of driving, they saw no people. Or no one living. They passed through villages, and all who could had fled, it seemed, or gone to earth; just a few animals straying, bewildered; scrawny goats scattering as Pohl and his men drove past. *This is what an army does, my Dorle. This is the aftermath.*

Well, what did you expect? Pohl imagined his wife's reply. *It is a war you've gone to, no?*

She never wanted him anywhere near it. Dorle told him as much before he came out here: *You needn't think I can approve of this.*

She can't lie to him: that's just the way she is, so Pohl knows how much it hurt her that he took this posting. But still he talks to her inside. When he wakes in the mornings, and when he lies down to sleep again; it helps him to think of home at the start and end of each working day. Pohl often finds himself talking to Dorle in between times too: at his desk, in the lulls at his site office, or in the solitude of his car. Even now, ploughing on through the fog, still overcome by this morning, feeling the shortness of his sleep and the sour lack of breakfast inside him, Pohl thinks that if he could be set apart with her, just for a short time, then it would surely help him. Because they talk things out, the pair of them: this is how they've always been.

Pohl had to talk and talk with her when they were courting, walk and walk with her. Fond as they were by then, she'd thought it too late for them to think of marrying. *Old friends and fossils:* that's what Dorle called them both. He was forty and past his prime years as a suitor; Dorle was not so much younger and accustomed to her own ways; *you know how I am by now.* She had long had her own clear-eyed look on life.

But for that boldness, her parents would have seen her married in her twenties, to a son of a solid Münster merchant, preferably, or one of the younger bachelors among her father's associates. When Dorle went to university, her mother despaired that she wasn't marrying material; and when she took up teaching after she graduated – her classes full of daughters from good Rheinland families just like her own one. But Dorle said she worked to keep herself, so she could please herself; beholden to no one, she had the long school holidays free to spend walking, or on endless card games at friends' apartments. Or just to spend idling: Dorle liked to read in the bathtub for hours at a time. She had time enough, she said, to do that, and for talking and laughing, and thinking her own thoughts, which was the best life had to offer. She told Pohl, smiling, that the two of them could talk their thoughts out loud with one another; had they not known each other since childhood days? What more could they ask? But that smile had been encouragement, and Pohl had wanted no other wife.

Dorothea deserves a sainthood, Pohl's brother-in-law wrote to him after their Emmy was born, only a year after the wedding. Such a solemn and pretty little baby, and such a surprise to both of them: they had expected companionship, not to be a family. Fossils no more, Dorle called them Abraham and Sarah instead, and she laughed over her family's confusion: joy and embarrassment in almost equal measure that the two of them should become parents when they were greying at the temples.

Pohl's brother-in-law told him to be careful not to land Dorle with another baby, *not at her age, and not when you might be enlisted, you should take care of my sister* – it irks

Pohl to remember. And to think that the man will soon be a father again himself, for the fourth time over. His wife will get a medal for this next child, bronze, the nearest thing to sainthood the Party confers; but Pohl knows Dorle has no such aspirations.

'Who has children for their sake?'

She is as sharp as a knife blade, and cuts just as cleanly; Dorle sees her many nephews as blessings, certainly, but not from the Führer.

'Does he presume such powers now?'

Time was, when friends came over in the evenings, they used to roll their eyes and shake their heads in shared contempt for the brown crowd who ruled them. Now, too many friends shrug their shoulders.

'What can we do? We are stuck for the meantime with this Führer.'

'Yes, we have to stick with him now it is wartime.'

'Remember the last war. That disaster.'

'No good ever came our way from losing.'

Make the best of a bad job, they say. And: *just until this is over*. And: *at least we have the Wehrmacht*.

'At least Hitler has the generals to guide him.'

But Dorle has no time for such contortions, for such distorted thinking: 'Who can put their faith in generals, I ask you, when they serve such criminals? Marching into Poland, into France now. Whatever next?'

She throws up her hands, after friends have left again, and it is just the two of them in the parlour chairs.

'Who is there left we can invite now? Who can we talk to without fuming?'

Dorle is scornful, and while Pohl has minded her to be careful (*if you talk of our esteemed leaders, then with the windows closed, please*) it gives him some of the succour he is craving, thinking of her forthright ways as he is driving; of his wife's plain-spoken disdain for the powers-that-be-now.

But if she knew what those powers are doing here?

Pohl takes a harder grip of the steering wheel.

He is on a marsh route that he's unfamiliar with; he has never driven this far before, but still he presses onwards. Only when he sees no more houses, no more field boundaries, does he begin to slow the car, relieved to be alone now. But despite the emptiness, his thoughts keep crowding in on him.

By the time friends were drafted – or friends volunteered, even – they'd already agreed, he and Dorle: he would not fight in service of the Party. The idea of this was intolerable.

So Pohl went from office to office with his petitions, sitting for hours on end in the draft bureau waiting rooms; all small-windowed and airless, designed to demoralise. But he persisted – taking his letters of reference and his engineering certificates, spreading out his neatly typed lists on the desks, when his turn was eventually called, naming all the roads and road-bridges he had worked on since he qualified.

The officials looked all his papers over, glancing up at the wire rims of his glasses, then down again at his prescription for short-sightedness (Dorle said he should leave nothing out: *leave nothing to chance*).

The officials narrowed their eyes at Pohl's lapels, too: his Party badge, conspicuous in its newness. This was his brother-in-law's contribution: *You can wear the blasted pin and keep your scruples; of course you can, you innocent.* (Pohl had begun to fear it might, in fact, be the only way left to keep them.)

The officials knew a flag of convenience when they saw it; they must have seen any number of front-avoiders decide to fly the swastika on sufferance. But they conceded all the same: Pohl would be more useful behind the lines.

The Party badge is still a sore point between him and Dorle. ('Tell me you haven't.' She gave him such a dark look, when he returned from taking her brother's counsel. 'Oh, tell me you haven't, please.') But the unease that comes over him now is about more than that; this creeping guilt is far worse. It has Pohl steering to the roadside, his tyres now sinking, now bumping, and then stopping the car entirely, sitting hunched and uncertain with the engine turning over. There is just so much about this place he hasn't told her.

Pohl could write so little of what he really felt in his early letters, he confined himself to practicalities. Telling Dorle how he and his men surveyed the land in the first weeks, and set up construction posts: large encampments, for materials and for labourers, at 15-kilometre intervals. Once enough of these were in place, the work gangs began quarrying a path, wide and level, excavating a trench through the rough lowlands.

The thoroughfare he is building is to be a grand one: Himmler has decreed it. But Pohl spared his wife the SS bombast, sticking to the engineers' brief he'd received with his contract: that the road should be wide enough for two-way traffic, and high enough to withstand winter flooding. *No small task in these wetlands, I can tell you.*

Heap a ton of rubble onto the mud here and, come the morning, it will have sunk without trace again; the mire forever sucking at the duckboards they have to lay and re-lay between the workers' quarters.

'Marsh' was amongst the first Ukrainian words Pohl learned here, simply through repetition. *Bolota, bolota.* The labourers blamed the swampy ground for all their building woes, and not without justification: a road in this terrain – at least a solid and even one, which is the only kind Pohl can allow himself – will be quite some test of his engineering skills. *But why come all this way to build something if you're not going to build it properly?*

You build it well then. If you must be out there.

Dorle's replies have confined themselves to the shortest and sorest of paragraphs; and Pohl knows he will not be able to talk it out with her until his next home leave comes – until construction here is nearing completion – and this seems such a long time.

But the backfilling has been successful. On the western-most stretches, the workers are already layering sand and gravel, bedding in the aggregate. Pohl's labour teams here will follow on, in due course; after they have finished digging out the drainage trenches and shoring up the embankments, they can begin preparing for the asphalt, finally; they can smooth their way through these new and vast territories.

It is a road for when this war is over. No more tanks will have to roll then. Pohl has told Dorle this, over and over – in his thoughts this time, not in his letters to her: that would be too dangerous. *It is for when Hitler loses, as he surely must, my love. Just look at all his over-reaching madness – the man means to conquer Russia now: I ask you! It can only be a matter of time.* Still aware of her soreness, and how his letters can do little to soothe it, Pohl has assured her repeatedly – even if only inwardly – that he has come to build a road here, good and broad, and fit for civilians. *Fit for civilisation, not some thousand-year abomination.* And even if he'd sooner tell her in person, it has still eased him to say these things.

It eased him too, when the people began returning out of hiding: farmers to their farms, peasants to the allotments they tended. Pohl told Dorle, so he would remember it all to tell her later, how they were still shaken at first, and cautious, after what they'd suffered under the retreating Russians. Pohl was shaken himself – by the rags they wore; by their weather-worn faces and toothlessness, old beyond their years; by their dirty and barefoot children. *Honestly, I am living among people from another century.* He didn't like, either, the onion stink of them (*if I am truthful, Dorle, as I know I always should be with you*). But it was a relief that the countryside he drove through from boarding house to roadworks was soon dotted again with people. Women greeting the morning with a scatter of grain and a cluster of hens at their ankles; the men, too, were early risers, already out at first light, carrying planks and adzes, making repairs, tilling the black earth.

Everything grows here, like you couldn't imagine. Sugar beet and winter wheat; Pohl drove out to the labour camps each morning through acres of dry-gold rye and barley, and the landscape that had seemed so flat and empty at first soon revealed itself as bountiful – a place of goat- and swineherds, and of ancient orchards under wide skies. In the peasants' gardens, the weeds were cleared again from potatoes and garlic – the latter in pungent over-abundance in all his boarding house evening meals, of course, but Pohl felt himself adjusting.

September was glorious; October began likewise, and he described the change of season for Dorle: the new cool of the mornings, the slow-turning yellow of the birch leaves. *There has even been a harvest; thanks be for the fields left untouched by the Soviets.* Farmhands strode through the crop into the evenings, and Pohl watched the steady swing of the scythe blades in the low sun as he returned from working to the town again. He saw whole families at the reaping: boys striding behind their fathers, children bending and gleaning, old women sitting companionable in the stubble, tying the stalks into sheaves to dry. And on Sundays, after waking late, Pohl walked at the riverside. *It's where they baptise their children; I wish you could see that.* All the children in the district, it seemed, were brought to the water; more every passing week, a streaming procession of families. Toddlers and ten-year-olds, wading hand in hand; babes-in-arms carried into the river's flow; all born under Stalin, only now allowed their immersion. *These people had so much denied them.*

It would take months, well into next spring, for the priests to reach the outlying villages; in the meantime, all those within walking distance went to the river services, rising long before dawn to bring their children to the water at long last. The priest stood in the shallows to receive them, the hems of his robes spreading pale across the river's surface, and his arms held out to his young charges. Solemn, ceremonious, he blessed them and he lifted them. *And how the people sing then, Dorle; if you could only hear them; the massed congregation on the riverbank*. Even days afterwards, just recalling this, Pohl found himself uplifted.

But it doesn't help him to remember this morning.

His hands gripped to the steering wheel to steady them, Pohl is still too appalled at what he saw outside his boarding-house window; at being witness to such brutality.

His Dorle was right about this posting. He should have tried harder, resisted longer. He will not fight in this war – but perhaps this is not enough to save him.

Ahead of him are the marshes. Partisan territory, still unconquered by his countrymen; Pohl can see it through the fog-held stillness. And he can see too, now, how Himmler's men have made full use of this.

The fighting is far to the east, the front troops are all well beyond Kiev, and Pohl had expected civil servants here by this time, Reich officials for all his dealings with the district offices. But, even now, the territory is under military rule.

No mere invaders, the SS have extended their duties in the district. It is not safe, Himmler claims, until the rule of law has been established, until the partisans have been flushed out of the marshland. So his men have taken charge of administration as well as patrolling – of construction too, for the meantime; putting together work gangs from the villages to build the new police quarters at the town's edge, and all the new offices for the civilian administration, yet to be posted here from Germany.

SS hands touch everything here. Even the roadworks.

It is they who find and provide the Ukrainian labour teams Pohl uses. They who deliver workers to the sandpits and the gravel pits and the quarries; men to break the stones and haul the rubble; and more men for the road encampments, to take instruction from the overseers.

It is not something Pohl feels easy with. Or that he has told his Dorle. He hunches further behind the windscreen, blinking out into the fog-shrouded nothingness.

It is less a road he has stopped on than a track, cutting northwards through rough country, and now the emptiness out here begins to unnerve him. The way ahead is pocked with holes and puddles, the ground on either side sodden. And if he drives much further, Pohl knows he will be in the marshes: no German welcome there, even a civilian.

He imagines the feeling – on his next leave, say – of sitting Dorle down in front of him. He thinks of the ugliness in what he must tell, in what she must hear him say out loud.

Our soldiers came for the Jews in the early hours.

Pohl wrenches the steering wheel, turning back sharply for the roadworks.

Yasia hears the siren first, a sudden burst of wailing noise, and then the crackle of a loudhailer: a German voice speaking in Ukrainian.

'. . . under the law of occupation.'

It sends the old horse shying beside her, and Yasia has to grasp the reins to halt him while the crows rise cawing from the treetops into the low clouds above them. Taking the animal's head, she stops him at the birches, under their winter-bare branches that mark the start of the town streets, the end of the fields and orchards – and there she listens a moment.

'. . . under curfew, until further notice. Movement is permitted in daylight hours only.'

The mist has the cobbles slick beneath her muddied boot-soles, and its cold beads are on the shawl wrapped about her head and shoulders, heavy with the damp of three hours' walking, from farm to market town, most of it still in darkness. Only the horse's breath is warm on Yasia's fingers as she puts a palm to his nose to soothe him, and the loudhailer keeps up its wailing. It is fading in and out now, dampened by the stone walls and the tight-packed houses, but always the same voice returning; Yasia lifts her head as it comes again.

'Gatherings of more than three people are not permitted on the town streets.'

Her father's old horse shifts, her mother's sacks of apples shifting with him, strapped across his bony flanks, and Yasia puts a staying hand to his neck, taking a tighter grip of the reins again.

She had to pull him the last mile or so on the walk here, where the mud was deepest, fog at its thickest; so taken up with clicking and cajoling, she'd stopped watching for the town spires in the mist, for any lamps lit in the windows, as she always does with her mother on market days.

It took Yasia aback when she saw no one at the fork, where the cart track merges with the first of the cobbled streets, and the going gets a little easier: traders usually gather there at the stone arch, the old town gateway, as they come in from the villages, and she was expecting to walk on to the market street among them. But then Yasia saw the jeeps passing, the Germans like shadows inside them. They cut across the street she'd meant to walk down, fleet and dark; they were there and then gone again – just like that blaring noise they make.

Yasia hasn't caught enough yet to know their reasons, but the soldiers are circling the place, she is sure of that much: they are making their presence felt here. And even now that they have passed her, and all is falling quiet, she isn't yet certain that it's safe enough to go further.

The horse drops his head to nose at her, the crows returning to their roosts among the branches, but Yasia sees the street ahead of her is shuttered and empty. The fog hangs between the houses, and a hush does too: movement is permitted, or so these soldiers say, but none of the townsfolk are taking them at their word.

She is on the boundary road that skirts the edge of the town. Looking along it, finding it deserted, Yasia turns the horse now, cautious, leaving the cover of the branches, thinking to make for Osip's workshop instead of the market street. His yard is on the outskirts – and Osip is family too. So Yasia thinks she'll be safest there, beyond the town hall, out by the railway sidings, until she knows why the Germans are turning their circles.

Yasia saw her first Germans in August.

Before that, they had Stalin.

'Ten years, my daughter.'

Her papa held both his palms up, all his fingers spread wide, so they could see how many they'd endured, when the final order came from the Collective.

'Those stooges.'

Her papa hated anyone who worked for the Soviets.

He was eating the breakfast she'd made him, sitting at the farm table with all her brothers, all of them younger, who she'd chased from their beds, and washed and fed, as she did every morning. Her mother was busy with the baby, still new and fretful; the oldest boys were sullen and sleepy and already in their field clothes; the many younger ones at Yasia's skirts, small limbs pressed to her and waiting.

'Ten years,' her papa told his children. 'But this is the worst one.'

All the collectives in the district had been told to bring in the harvest, though it was barely July. They were to work day and night, if need be. Or destroy the crop: pour paraffin on the fields and burn them. *Leave nothing for the Germans.*

'What have the Germans done to us, I ask you? It's the Communists I'd set fire to,' her papa declared. 'I'd walk away and leave them burning.'

Yasia's many brothers looked at their father blankly. She did too: her papa had always toed the line, more or less silently, until then.

Years ago, perhaps half her lifetime, Yasia remembered her father's evening mutterings about the village elders. Her brothers were already sleeping, all those who'd been born by then, but Yasia had sought out her mother's solid form to curl against, because those were hungry times. Her mama rocked the cradle at the stove-side with her toes, and her papa muttered and stoked the flames while he called the Farm Chairman spineless. *Weak-willed, weak-minded.* All the names he could think of. *He blows with the wind, that man; he bends wherever he sees advantage.* Her mama nodded, emphatic, Yasia felt her. Especially when her papa spoke of their land being stolen from under them: *harvests meant for our children's mouths, stolen to feed Russian brats.* Her father spoke his mind back then, in mutters at least, at the stove-side in the evenings. But Yasia knew that, in daylight, he did as he was bidden. *He doesn't bend with the wind, your father, but he bends under the yoke, child*; that's what her mother said about him, while her papa found less and less to say. Over the years he became a silent man.

So it surprised all his children to hear him announce his disobedience.

'I will not destroy the crop I have planted.'

'Yes, Papa.'

And to see him spit Stalin's name in the dirt as he was leaving the yard.

'What is our papa saying, Yasia?'

'Where is our papa going, big sister?'

'You all be quiet now.'

Yasia hushed them, watching him stride out to the pasture. But as soon as he was out of earshot, she sent her own curse to Moscow, to fly alongside her father's.

She had her own reasons.

Yasia would have been a wife a year already, were it not for Joseph Stalin. She should have been married, been a mother. Instead, she had turned seventeen without the young husband, and without the fat baby she was so sure she'd be cradling this summer, as plump and soft as her mama's many baby boys. Yasia had not seen her Mykola since he was drafted; her sweetheart had been lost to the Red Army, and though she tried just then, following her father's example, she found no curse loud enough or harsh enough to compensate.

The Farm Chairman was at the yard gate the following morning.

The new day already hot and damp, promising a deluge, he stood dabbing at his face with his shirt tails, panting the latest. In the next village – Mykola's village – they were up in arms. They were disobeying orders. More: they were taking back their fields, even taking back their tools so no one else could use them.

'They are breaking up the Collective. Overnight. They decided. Who on earth gave them the authority?'

The Farm Chairman threw up his palms and told them he'd been cycling from homestead to homestead since daybreak, to consult the remaining farmers:

'And you, Fedir?' he entreated.

Yasia's father pulled on his boots in answer, and set off for the village while the Farm Chairman followed him down the puddled lane, imploring: 'But please, please, my friend, take back only what is yours.'

Her papa was home by midday, flushed, triumphant, with his horse and his ploughshares, which had not stood in their barn since Yasia was a child.

'Do you remember, my daughter?'

'I do, Papa.'

So rare to see her father satisfied, her father smiling; the sight of that had her brothers staring, as much as the belongings returned to them.

Her mother was certain it was the Lord's work: 'He has mercy on us after all.'

But Yasia couldn't share in her rejoicing. Because why had the Lord, in all his mercy, not returned her Mykola?

She knew herself selfish, but she couldn't help it. Yasia thought daily of the old crone in a headscarf she might become without him. Or worse: the old man she might have to marry, if all the young men should perish now at the hands of the Germans; so many had perished already for the Soviets.

The old men in the district divided the grain the next morning, all the crops still in the ground, and the hayricks between them. In just a short day's back and forth, IV Stalin Collective Farm was no longer, the record books consigned by her papa to the kitchen stove.

He stirred the embers, gratified, but he muttered to Yasia and her mother: 'No celebrating; not yet.'

He would let no one tempt that devil fate.

They were lucky in the end. Their farmstead was not near the main route east, the main line of retreat. It was Mykola's village that caught the worst of it: Red Army foot troops passed through there. Turning tail in the face of the Germans, they turned on the farms, going through the barns, breaking up the ploughs, the hayforks and the harrows.

Out in the fields, they went from stack to stack with torches, setting the hayricks blazing, and the last of the beet crop that Mykola's grandfather hadn't brought in.

His cows were driven out too, from the milking pen into the burning pasture; beaten across their hindquarters, and set running through the flames.

Yasia stood in the yard with her mother that afternoon, all her brothers around them, watching the smoke plumes rising, grey-purple on the near horizon. She could still see the glow of the fires come the evening; they were burning as Yasia climbed into bed beside the younger ones, so she knew the flames must have caught the buildings. And then she was woken by Grandfather's cows at first light, blundering through the yard. Stinking of bonfire, too exhausted, too frightened to return home; udders swollen and sore, they bellowed to be milked in the cool morning air.

Yasia learned, then, how it was to feel fury. Before, she had been frightened. For Mykola mainly, called away to do Stalin's bidding; for her papa too, and what any foot troops left might do to him: he had penned the cows and then set off across the fields to help the villagers.

But the troops had already done with the place and departed, and her papa returned smoke-blackened with Mykola's sister by the hand; he found Myko's mother and grandfather in the hours that followed. And in the weeks that came after, they sat up long into the nights, telling of all they had seen, and worse, all that they had heard since.

The rail lines to the town had all been dynamited, and the signal boxes too. *The same in Kiev*, Myko's sister whispered – but of Kiev there was so much more to tell. Whole districts were being looted, and what they couldn't carry, the Russians were burning, or just ruining: sacks of sugar, sacks of leather, even packs of medicines they threw into the Dnieper. In Zhytomyr, the Komsomol burned down the bread factory. *Such criminality.* To burn bread and the grain that made it, the grain of so many hands' harvest. And still no word, still no word from Mykola.

'We must brace ourselves,' his grandfather told them: the German invasion had yet to reach them.

When she heard the *Luftwaffe* planes drone, Yasia was crossing the pasture, her father's lunch pail in one hand, and the youngest of her brothers clutched to the other. Too far from the barn, from the farmhouse, they had nowhere to run, nowhere to shelter. So she scooped up Oleksiy and laid him beside her in the grass, their faces pressed to the damp earth, her father's milk spilled across her skirts.

But they dropped no bombs that day, the Germans; only showers of paper. Leaflets that littered the verges, sticking limp in the crop after the afternoon downpour.

The German planes had scattered Ukrainian words, and Yasia read these out loud for her father, after the planes were gone, and the worst of the rain too: she and Oleksiy found him on the pasture's far side, catching at the papers blowing across the grass, and he thrust the wet tatters at Yasia to decipher.

We have no quarrel with those who lead a peaceful life, with those who wish Ukraine to prosper.

She had been taught just enough at the Collective school to make out that much.

'Read more. What does that say? And that part?' Her papa pointed, impatient, even eager now. 'Read on, my daughter. What else do the Germans say?'

The words she found there made Yasia's chest tight.

We have no quarrel with men who were drafted, with any who lay down Soviet arms of their own free will now.

Each damp leaflet a free pass for Red Army deserters. If Mykola found one, he had only to present himself.

All over the district, mothers and sisters found reason to hope there. Children were sent running out with fistfuls of the gathered German papers to find fathers and uncles and cousins, while the menfolk emerged, blinking, from their hiding places in the grain bins and distillery cellars.

And then, finally, after so long praying and waiting; dusk

was just falling, lamps being lit in the farmhouse kitchen, when they caught sight of a caller, dust-covered, by the well in the yard.

Oleksiy pointed out of the window and asked: 'Who is that man?'

'Oh!'

'Oh, who do you think, child?'

So much thinner than before; he was properly gaunt from his long walk, from all his months of poor Red Army rations. Her poor Mykola.

His shoulder blades like sharp wings under his shirt, Yasia saw them as his mother flung open the door to him, and his raw-boned leanness had her tongue-tied, newly shy of him somehow, as his sister ran to pull him inside. Yasia had to steal away, though it shamed her; she had to retreat a while to swallow her shock, to still her heart, stealing glances at him through the knot holes in the wooden farmhouse walls, while Myko sat hunched and dripping in the tin bath his mother poured.

Washed clean again in the water she'd warmed, he sat at the table; Yasia put food in front of him, plate after plate, and this helped her, even if he ate so little, only drinking the beer she poured him; she found she could stand at Mykola's elbow while his grandfather sat talking, talking.

Mykola's mother and his sister sat with him too, recounting their woes, describing the charred barn and ruined beet crop, and the cows that gave no milk now: the sorry mess that was all they had left them.

Mykola said little. 'Yes, I saw it.' He told them he'd walked through the village on his way here.

He must have walked and walked through other towns and villages just like it; too many ruined places; Yasia could see that from the hollows of his cheeks and temples, the sore drooping of his reddened eyelids. Still Myko's family talked on, relentless. Until he put his head down and slept, sudden and face-down on the table, between his plate and beer glass.

But after everyone was sleeping, Mykola woke again; he came and stole her from her bed, and he lay with her in the orchard grass.

She had lain with him there before. Yasia had first known Myko before he was a soldier, when he was a boy and blond as wheat, come to help her father with the harvest. Her father couldn't know, so they had to be careful – they were not even nearly old enough to marry then – so they'd hidden themselves among the old trees, in the long grass; far from the pasture and the farmhouse. And then they'd lain there, unbuttoned, their breath held, both of them; pressed together and hushed, lest they be discovered and this would have to stop, this press of him against her. Brown and gold after a day in the fields, chaff from the threshing caught in the down on his upper lip, it was his boy's blunt fingers Yasia remembered most, reaching inside her dress, his eyes intent. He'd pressed his palms to her belly first, eager, uncertain, so Yasia had pulled them to her breasts; she'd pulled them where she wanted them, and she'd lifted her skirts for him.

This time it was different. Myko was no longer so clumsy, so inexpert; neither did he lie wrapped around her afterwards. And Yasia lay awake then, blinking at the back of his sleeping head beside hers. This Mykola, she thought, was not her Mykola of old.

But his sleeping face was still a boy's, when she sat up and looked at him; his eyes closed, soft mouth open, just the way he'd always slept.

He was home, and he was safe. And he still wanted to lie with her in the orchard. Yasia thought she would feed him and they would lie here, and soon he would speak again, as he used to. Soon she would be his bride too.

So when the first German land troops arrived, she had bread and salt ready for them.

Mykola's grandfather saw her baking, and he told her he would only wave to a German soldier to wave him on his way again.

'No more invaders.' He shook his head at her and the loaves she'd made. 'What our good country needs now is good Ukrainians.'

But Yasia's father saw her too, and after the old man went into the yard, he said she didn't have to mind him. Her papa had tended the cows with Mykola's mother ever since the farm was burned; they had to share the milking and the herding, because Grandfather couldn't or wouldn't be relied upon. He spent all his days sitting and smoking, still shocked and muttering over his losses, and Yasia knew her papa found it hard to stomach that. *We all have to get on with our lives.*

She walked out early, in any case, with Myko's sister and all the youngest boys: Yasia took them long before the menfolk were awake and could do any arguing. So they were there at the roadside, a small and young crowd of them, waiting with gifts when the *Wehrmacht* convoys came riding.

They came in jeeps and on motorbikes, plastered with the black mud thrown up by their tyres. Did they not realise? These lands below the marshes, they are good for horseback only, or foot travel; for sledges in winter, impassable after summer storms. The tracks here were either mire or dust or snowdrifts – not meant for taking at lightning speed – and Yasia laughed behind her hand with Mykola's sister, about how little these Germans knew of the country they had conquered in their *Blitzkrieg*: perhaps Grandfather was right after all, and they should just wave the soldiers on again?

But the Germans had phrasebooks; words they had memorised from so many repetitions as they'd crossed the countryside.

'Hey, girls! Miss!' They called to them, these dirt-streaked and motorised invaders, who seemed to her to be liberators – bringers-back of her husband-to-be, their orchard secrecy; all her hopes of motherhood too.

Mud-bespattered, they halted at the roadside, pulling off their helmets and smiling.

'Bolshevik finished,' they told her. 'Now Ukraina.' Wiping their foreign and well-fed faces.

'Ukrayeena,' Yasia corrected.

She saw how they looked at the swing of her skirts, and at the brown roundness of her calves, pleased by what they'd found here; all eyes on the open buttons at her blouse neck. And Yasia knew that she could please men this way, and easily, but she would not flirt, because she was as good as married now, of course.

'Ukrayeena.'

She told them, firm; one brother at her hand, another at

her hip, like the young mother she would be soon enough. And the soldiers grinned at her as they rode off eastwards.

Others are here now. More of their number, circling the town streets – and none of them are friendly.

Yasia hears the jeeps returning as she reaches Osip's workshop: they are still streets away, but their sirens echo shrill across the rooftops as she ducks along the lane walls.

Yasia rattles at Osip's yard gate, flinging a handful of gravel at his shuttered windows. She took a wrong turning coming in from the outskirts to find him, and the place looks so different with all the streets empty, Osip's grey head comes as a relief, the bulk of him too, as he opens the gate, finally. Just a crack, just enough to peer through.

'Oh! It's you, girl.'

His eyes widen at seeing a family face. But the frown lines around them are dark.

'What have you come for?' he asks, although Yasia has stayed here so often before.

A little fatter, a little greyer even than the last time she saw him, he throws anxious glances at her muddied skirt hems and the sacks of apples she bound so hastily across the horse's back this morning. But then the loudhailer comes blaring, and he pulls her inside, tugging the horse and its burden after her.

'Did your mother send you? Does your father know?' Osip hurries her – and then he hushes her straight after: 'Not now – not so loud, girl. Don't you hear them?'

He points behind his shoulder, as if at the sirens' wailing, closing the yard gate swiftly behind himself.

'Only safe inside,' he cautions, and he pulls Yasia further, into the shelter of his workshop doorway.

Around her, all is as always: Osip's low house, just across the yard bricks; his workshop behind her, with its smell of resin and sawdust. But even among his tools and benches and broken cart wheels, the familiar mess here, Yasia sees how Osip glances, nervous, up at the house fronts rising above his yard walls; she sees all those shuttered windows, and Yasia thinks of how many townsfolk must be crouched and listening behind them.

Then the loudhailer barks again: ' . . . under curfew under further notice.'

The jeeps pass far too close beyond the yard walls, and she stands with Osip as the voice announces: 'Anyone flouting this order will be taken prisoner. Will be removed from here. Under the law of occupation.'

So Yasia hears now: the Germans haven't only come giving orders, they have come to take as well. They take whatever they want, whoever they have use of. Who have they come for?

3

The schoolmaster has not moved yet.

He is still on the floor where he landed, where Ephraim laid him – as carefully as he could without the guards getting angry. And Ephraim stands as still as he can now, holding vigil over the old man.

He has stood here for a long time, silent, with his wife beside him and their youngest, their small Rosa. With the schoolmaster at their feet, on the cold brick of the factory floor.

Miryam stands firm, Ephraim can feel her: dark hair knotted, coat collar buttoned, Rosa's small hand in her own, keeping her upright. But with each new arrival, the crowd has become pressed more tightly around them, and each time it shifts now, Ephraim has to check on the doors first, to see who is pushed in, and then on the old man: that he still has space around him, and he is still breathing; that his condition has not worsened.

Ephraim is mindful, both of the schoolmaster's welfare and to keep the doorway in his eyeline – so that he can see the face of each new person brought in. But there are long and painful lulls to contend with, where all he can do is wait here for the next arrival; wait and wait in amongst this crush of people. So mostly he finds it is easier to keep his eyes closed, not to take in his surroundings, not to believe that this is happening. The whispers tell him anyway: all the uncertainty he hears, and the resentment.

'It is a ghetto, I tell you.'

'Yes, it is a *ghetto* they will take us to.'

They are so pressed together, all the Jews from the lands below the marshes; Ephraim is with all of his own kind, and they are made to stand, all of them: the old and ill too, as well as the children. All except the schoolmaster. He is allowed to lie still, recover from the blows. Small mercy, but it is a mercy all the same, and Ephraim keeps expecting it to be extended to the schoolmaster's mother, because it should be extended, surely: her son is injured, and she is too old for this.

Ephraim has felt her bending, again and again, as though to sit by him. She does not understand why they must stand and stand here, and so she tries to sit – she has tried repeatedly – but then Miryam has pulled her gently, persistently, to her feet again, minding her: *Careful, careful of the guards.*

They must be careful, Ephraim thinks, not to whisper reproaches, as so many around them do; not to draw attention.

'This is what I think of their resettlement.'

There has been far too much whispering, all through the long hours while it was still dark outside, and when the light began rising; and every fresh wave of murmur, of rumour, has given him new cause to be anxious. He wants to know what awaits them as much as anyone, but all these whispers are unsettling; any noise makes him nervous. So now, as the loudhailer calls return, Ephraim feels himself shrinking, even as he strains his ears to pick up the announcements.

' . . . the curfew in force, from sun-up to sun-down.'

The inflection is strange, but the words are still loud enough to be made out above the blaring, above the vehicle engines.

'Movement is permitted, but for work purposes only.'

German jeeps, he thinks, and German trucks: in his mind's eye, he sees them; so many Germans inside them.

' . . . found hiding Jews, or supplying partisan gangs, or supporting . . . '

It is such a bellowing noise they make, Ephraim has found himself shrinking back, despite himself, each time they have passed this morning. And they pass again now – for the fourth time? The fifth time? – beyond the factory, their noise receding again as they take the turning.

' . . . punished accordingly, under the law of occupation.'

Ephraim knows the town's streets so well he can picture the route they are taking: right now, the Germans will be driving over the ruts and flagstones along the northern boundary, and they will keep on going until they get to the old bridge, where they will have completed another of their circuits.

'... repeat, for work purposes only ...'

The noise of them, still just audible, has stopped the whispering for the meanwhile. It stopped the whispers last time too, as all the people stood and listened to the announcements, hoping for any hint of what might be coming next for all of them. It sounded like so many trucks were passing, the noise of their engines set off a new and swiftly spread conviction: surely these are the trucks the Germans have brought to take them?

'But where will they take us?'

'Why must they make us wait, then?'

The people around Ephraim cannot help but fret about how long all this is taking, because it is too cold, and the waiting is intolerable. It leaves them with too much to worry over: if they have taken enough food for the journey, enough clothing?

'How long will they keep us here to freeze?'

'Soon, they will take us. Soon, I can feel it.'

Ephraim understands their fretting. But still, he is fearful that the silence he now stands in will be replaced again before long by more such anxious speculation. He is not ready for leaving; he is not ready, so he cannot abide all this talk of it. Talk of being taken only serves to unnerve him, as does any shifting he hears around him.

Last time, the silence that followed the vehicles was broken not by talking, but by the scuffing of cloth against concrete; the rasp of a bundle of clothing, pushed steadily – by a foot, most probably – inch by inch towards the schoolmaster. The noise was so close, Ephraim felt certain the foot must be his wife's, it must be Miryam's, though he kept his face stiffly forward, so as not to alert the guards. *She should do nothing to alert them.* Ephraim did not see his wife do the pushing, but he did see her, out of the corner of his eye, when she bent swiftly and pressed the bundle under her old teacher's nape. It was to support his head, to let him rest – Ephraim knows his Miryam well, and what she would be thinking. And perhaps it even worked, because this is what woke him, the old schoolmaster: this kindness. The soft rasp of the bundle first, then the lifting of his cheek from the cold brick beneath it. Miryam brought him round, briefly, allowed him to rest a little more comfortably.

But then came shouting; the sharp rap of coshes on the iron doors, and the barked order to stand still.

'Stand upright! As you were told to.'

The start this gave Ephraim was painful. It sharpened his fears, too; had him blinking and squinting again towards the doorway, through the few gaps in the people surrounding him. He has heard this noise so often this morning; he's even counted the guards who make it: four of them, all told, making themselves broad in their police uniforms. He knows there are many more guards, many more soldiers still outside, searching the town. He knows the Germans will search out all of them.

And that shutting his eyes will not stop them.

It is light on the factory floor by now; it is bitter cold too, and when Ephraim opens his eyes properly, he sees his breath comes in clouds. It is the same for the breath of all those in here, so now he can watch the whispers as they pass from head to head around him; clouds of rumour passing from one group to the next.

'They will take us to a ghetto in trucks.'

'But they must find us all first.'

'Don't you have all your people? Who is still missing?'

'Who is not with you?'

Ephraim has seen many of his customers in here already; the backs of their heads enough to alert him, their winter hats, the curve of the frames he made them hugging familiar ears.

He recognises their voices, too. Because people do not only whisper, they call as well, now and again, across the crowd around them; whenever they dare, whenever the guards allow this, they call out to friends and family, checking they are in here.

'Binya?' Someone takes a chance. 'Binya? Are you here now?' And then, from the far side: 'Tomas? Tomas Ribchov?'

'Yevgeny, Marta.'

'Marta, dear? Riva?'

The calling of names rises, the voices with them, in tones of growing urgency, which fall away again as the crowd shifts, uneasy.

Not too much. That's enough now. We'll only make the guards angry.

The calling has risen and then fallen with every new set of people pushed onto the factory floor this morning; there are always new groups, new people chased out of hiding.

First comes running and shouting, out in the corridor, then the opening of the doors, and with that comes the awful feeling of more people falling – it seems to Ephraim each time that they are falling inside to join them. Sometimes it is a handful, sometimes it is whole families. Once there came twenty or even thirty new faces, all unfamiliar to him: a whole village cleared of its Jews, perhaps, all calling and crying out to one another for reassurance. For a while the guards allowed this, then they banged on the doors for silence.

Ephraim has searched and searched, each time, for faces dear to him. He knew the schoolmaster, as soon as he saw him stumbling, and he knows his customers. But he doesn't know any Binyas, any Ribchovs or Martas. There must be a hundred, two hundred Jews in here he's never met before. More all the time.

He and Miryam have been pressed and pushed with their Rosa, forced further and further from the doorway with every new set to join them. They have lost the schoolmaster and his mother in the crush, and then found them again – thankful for such mercies. Miryam has made sure to hold the old woman's hand now, as they have been forced to stand ever closer, pressed up against strangers, watching their clouds of breath, listening to their whispers, to their crying and their calling and then falling into anxious silence.

'Liba. My Liba dear?'

That call came an hour ago; the cloud of breath just a few heads away.

'Here, Papa! We are over here.'

Thanks be. It was such a relief to hear a call answered. Although Ephraim didn't know this Liba or her family, he felt the lift it gave them, and all those around him.

We cannot go, you see? he wanted to tell them. *Not until we have everyone here, every one of us.* And for a while that morning, each new set of captives saw another family completed, or so it seemed to him.

'You have the children? You have them?'

'Yes, Mama, yes! We are all together now.'

Each answering call was met with a rustle of movement, of bags and of children pressed ahead through the crush of people, following the sound or a hand raised, a handkerchief waved. And this is what has sustained him: Ephraim saw them waiting, just like him, and then he saw them reunited.

So each time the doors opened, Ephraim has called too. For his two sons, his two boys, still missing.

'Yankel?'

His voice so loud in the quiet.

'Yankel and Momik?'

They should have come by now; they should have been found. Although he feared what the SS might do to them, he still felt the boys should be here – with him and with Miryam.

So Ephraim called out as loud as he dared. Feeling the surge of hope, high and tight in his chest, that this calling gave rise to. And that surge of fear, too, sharp and painful, that they'd been hurt by the Germans.

He's seen – all too clearly – how often those pushed in here are injured; he can hardly look at the bruise, spreading blue and slow across the schoolmaster's jaw below him.

'Yankel and Momik? Speak if you are here now, my Yankel,' Ephraim has entreated, each time the door opened, with Miryam silent, breath held and listening beside him.

But there has come no answer. No shout, no sign of them coming through that doorway.

Where are they? Where are they?

For a long time now, there has been only waiting, and only whispering to fill it. The doors have not opened; there have come no more people.

Still, Ephraim keeps his eyes open. He knows Miryam is vigilant also, and this is some comfort: his wife standing firm beside him, hoping for their two sons. They cannot leave without them – Ephraim cannot even think of it – so he watches the doors, just as Miryam does, and he will keep on watching.

'Hurry, girl.'

Osip sends Yasia up the ladder in his workshop, into the low room above, strewn with straw bales, where she sleeps with her mother on market days.

The last jeeps passed a while ago, and Yasia doesn't know if the patrols are over, or how long they've been waiting either, but Osip wants to find out – and to be sure of the curfew hour – so she peers through the window, pane rippled with age, frame set deep into the stone wall, looking for the town-hall clock as he instructed.

'Can you see it?' Osip calls again, from below on his work-shop floor.

It hasn't struck all morning; not even the bell-ringer is out. Yasia can't see the face, just the tall shape of it in the fog, beyond the roof tiles of the houses. But the grey is lifting, so it must already be late morning; and she feels Osip's impatience, so she is quick about stowing the blankets he gave her and clambering down again to join him.

The horse is in the stall in his workshop corner. Osip has

untied the sacks, lifting them off the animal's back. But he won't let Yasia do more now.

'No time for that.'

He still won't say much, or let her ask questions, he only tells Yasia, low, that she can see about the horse, about the apples later.

'We have to see about the lie of the land first.'

One blunt finger pressed to his mouth in warning, he leads her out into the yard again; ducking through the crumbling brickwork in the wall behind his workshop, winding ahead of her through the narrow alleys between the houses.

Osip keeps far from any main streets, just in case, avoiding the few lanes they cross, cutting past and even across the neighbouring courtyards; Yasia has to trot to keep pace with him between the chicken sheds and piles of stove-wood, until they get to the right one.

Rough-hewn timbers are stacked shoulder high behind a small house, and Osip leads Yasia between them to the back door, warning: 'You have to know who is safe now. But the timber man is a good neighbour.'

And then he pulls her into the timber man's kitchen, dark and warm and thick with tobacco smoke. The place is thick with people.

Yasia has to press herself through wet wool jackets and low-voiced exchanges. No one is outside; still no one dares. Yasia thinks half the neighbourhood must be crowded inside here, and in their mutterings, she hears that all their talk is of the soldiers.

'They came through the whole town this morning.'

'Who could see that coming?'

'I knew nothing. Nothing, I tell you. Until those bastards woke me.'

They don't say who was taken, but Yasia feels their alarm as she weaves between them, seeing the way they lean into one another, all their mutterings urgent. She thinks the whole town must have woken when the soldiers came, peering fearful through their shutters, the gaps between their curtains. Then Osip takes her by the shoulders and pulls her to a stop at the table.

A woman sits at the head of it: the timber man's wife, it must be. Her arms full, her lap dripping children, she has a baby bound to her in its swaddling, a girl on her knee, and another smaller one, just old enough to stand, half-climbing up to join them.

'Osip! Here you are!' The woman holds out a hand. 'Sit, why don't you? And you,' she tells Yasia too, 'sit with us,' spilling her eldest off her lap to stand a moment.

She pours each of them a cup from the jug before her, and while stools are pulled up, while room is made at the table, Yasia's shawl is tugged back from her forehead.

'What a day to have a visitor!'

'She picked a fine time.'

The townsmen speak to Osip, not to her, but this is how it always is with the people here.

There are many faces Yasia knows around the table – by sight, if not by name – from market days. But there are many more she doesn't, and she feels herself flushing. She is never too sure of townsmen; *they never look, they only stare*, that's what her mother says about them. So Yasia pulls her shawl about herself, covering over her plaits again, just as her mother would, and then she shifts a little closer to Osip's bulk.

He is a cousin of sorts, on her mother's side, so Osip isn't really a townsman, or not a born one in any case, and while he does the talking, Yasia knows she can just sit quiet beside him. All the talk of soldiers has made her uncomfortable; the thought of them coming here and taking; and she keeps her gaze low, away from the staring faces, her eyes straying to the children: that lap-full of daughters at the head of the table.

One is still reaching, still waiting for a pause in her mother's talk and gesture, stubby fingers stretching out for her mother's embraces, and Yasia thinks the girl wants this talk to stop as much as she does.

'Have you come for wood?' The wife turns to Osip, pushing away her daughter. 'You can't have! You can't have, not after this morning. Stay,' she urges.

'Just for a short while.' Osip signals to her husband. 'I just want to hear the latest. Before I go about my business.'

'But who on earth can think of working?'

'Not me. I will not lift a finger,' one man asserts. 'Not while those bastards are still in the town here.'

But he says this last a little too loudly, because the timber man's daughter starts crying at the angry sound of him. Her mother pulls her closer, lifting the baby to make room for her, only this one cries in turn; it does not want to be lifted. So then the wailing gets all the louder, and all the talk is interrupted, while the baby is taken from its mother's arms to be quietened.

'Just wait, child.'

Wet mouth wide in protest, it is passed hand to hand until it reaches Yasia.

'You hold her,' she is told. 'You stop her crying.'

Townspeople never ask, they always order. Yasia has to push herself back from the table. But although she resents being pushed around like this, the small heft pressed into her lap smells of sleep and stove, just like her brothers, and it fits against her just as they do.

The voices pick up again around her. But Yasia thinks the townsmen can just go on with their soldier talk without her; she doesn't mind it so much now she feels the weight to be cradled, the small fingers gripped around her own ones. By the time the child has settled, and Yasia turns her thoughts back to the table, she finds the talk has turned to the people the Germans came for.

'They took my neighbour. Poor fool. And he said that they wouldn't.'

'Oh, mine too, mine too. But he had it coming. He was always too sure of himself.'

'That's what the Germans say about all of them.'

'So did they take all our yids?' a man at the stove asks. 'Or only some of them?'

Yasia knows little of Jews; nothing to speak of. There are none who farm with her father, or in Mykola's village either. All she's learned has been from folk tales, or overheard from townsfolk – but Yasia lifts her head to listen, because why would the Germans come after them?

'My neighbour was sleeping when the soldiers started.'

'He would have done better to be ready for them. They should have been ready, no? All of them.'

Townsmen are nodding now; Yasia sees them, all around the table.

'My neighbour did so well for himself. Always. Too well when we had Stalin.'

She has heard this last before. And not only about the Jews. It has come from her father's mouth about the Farm Chairman, and also from Myko's grandfather about his nearest neighbours – after they'd packed their cart and fled eastwards. *They always knew which way to point their faces.* Such hard-bitten complaints; Yasia has heard so many since the Soviets left. Once the Communists fled or lost their standing, ten years of hard feelings no longer had to be bitten back, and so Yasia listens to the back and forth, all the time thinking how the Farm Chairman bent with the wind, he bent wherever he saw advantage, so perhaps there is something in what the townsfolk say about the yids too.

'That one was in the Komsomol – remember?'

'And then on the town council.'

'Yes, that's right, that's right. I'd forgotten that about him.'

'So, then,' the man at the stove interrupts them. 'Was it only those Jews the Germans came for?'

Yasia turns to look, along with others at the table, because that's the second time he's cut in, and it was loud enough this time to have the room falling quiet.

'What do you care?' A woman next to Osip breaks the silence.

'I'm just saying.' The man at the stove puts his palms out, acting the innocent, while Osip's table-neighbour points a finger.

'Well, you always say too much,' she tells him. 'You hear me?'

'But I'm just asking,' the stove man counters. 'Just wondering where the Germans will take them. What use do they have for so many yids now?'

'What do I care?' the woman's answer comes sharply. 'They are only Jews. Why should we care about that?'

This last receives more nods, all around the kitchen: a murmured chorus of agreement.

Then: 'No, no, we should all be mindful.'

This is the timber man's wife.

'What use do the Germans have for any of us?' She halts the arguing. 'Why did they come to our town in the first place? That's what we should all be asking ourselves.'

She has them all quiet again – all thinking – Yasia can see that; how the woman's neighbours wait for her to go on.

'They came for a family just across the lane there.' The wife gestures, and then she pulls her arms around her daughters, saying the noise was so close it woke her. 'So loud, the soldiers. They were so loud, I tell you. I thought they were downstairs. Inside my house.' She pauses.

It still has her shaking; Yasia can see the tight way she holds her children, and the relief in her face that she was not taken, or her husband.

'We are all on their lists now, you know that.'

The woman looks in turn at all the faces at her table, at half the neighbourhood gathered in her kitchen, Yasia included; and the way she does this, slow and deliberate, keeps them all hushed and listening to her.

'So who is next?' she demands. 'After the *zhyds*, I mean. That's what we should ask now.'

This is too much for some.

'Don't talk so loud,' her husband tells her.

'Don't talk so much,' the woman is told too, by another sitting opposite.

All the assembled glance about themselves: at one another first, then at the doorway, the windows. No one wants the Germans hearing.

'There are still Germans everywhere this morning,' Osip reminds them all, low and frowning, hands wrapped around his mug.

And then the whispers start again.

'Are they still looking? The soldiers?'

'They must be.'

'But they won't take us, the Germans. They're not going to do that.'

'No, no. It's only the yids they want. The yids still hiding.'

The people turn back to the Jews again; easier to talk about Jews than one another.

'Yes, it's only the Jews they're after. The Germans can't abide them.'

But sitting quiet among them, holding the timber man's daughter, Yasia feels the girl's mother must be right, surely. She is on a list too, after all; and her father and mother and brothers. And so is Mykola.

Come to the new registration office: both families had got the order, so they all walked into the town one morning. Everyone in the district queued and queued there, in the September sun on the main square; sent from line to line until they got the right one, because the Germans insisted: everyone should be on the correct list.

The Germans had brought in army clerks to complete the task, to sit at desks ranked across the flagstones in the sun, inking the people onto their index cards.

The Jews stood in their own queue, Yasia remembers, and they each got a white armband to wear, even the children. So you could see who was a yid, then – and just how many there were.

Did you know there were so many?

I always said so.

Yasia stood with the people from the villages, listening to their murmurings; she stood there for hours, dutiful, with her mother and father and all her brothers, waiting to be catalogued and counted. *Name and age, occupation? Any religion, young Fräulein? Any illnesses? Your origins?* They even brought in translators from Kiev; the new authorities were diligent about completing their census.

Her mother's entry took the longest: sounding out her maiden name, and the name of the village she was born to, so small and sodden, the marsh smallholding where she spent her girlhood. Yasia's mama lived far from the town then, far from everything, before she married onto the drier land. Yasia's uncle still grazed his handful of cows on the boggy ground, growing what he could to feed himself, little more. *Small wonder he has no wife, no children*: Yasia's father often laughed about him, when he came up in conversation. He laughed about her uncle's solid face and slow way of talking, and his plough that was already old in Egypt. Yasia knew her mother didn't like this; she knew too, that she shared her mother's grey-green marsh eyes, her mother's broad marsh features, and she felt it in the German clerk's glances, noting the width of her mother's hips and cheekbones, and then her own ones. On market days, townsfolk buying their apples often took Yasia for a marsh girl, instead of the farmer's daughter she knew she was.

But then there they were, all together on the same list: all her family under the same name – her father's father's, who'd farmed their good land before him. It had come as a relief somehow to see them all set down there.

Yasia had caught sight of Myko around noon, standing in one of the furthest queues, with his grandfather beside him, and all the other men from his village; men he often stood with in those September days. All of them restless, faces dark, eyes sharp, heads bent together in talking: of what had befallen them, of what could be done until their farms were rebuilt, until a new crop was raised and reaped. How were they to house themselves, their families? How was it possible to feed and clothe them through the coming winter months?

Myko had come home only later, when the sun was long gone and Yasia had put all the younger ones to bed – she'd been watching for him such a long while. His tread slow across the yard, his eyes no longer so hard: she saw they had been washed soft, washed blank with alcohol. But Mykola had a good meal inside him. And a new armband too. Not white like the yids'; it was blue and yellow, the colours of her country, and he took it from his pocket to show her. Myko told her he'd be wearing it until he got his uniform, and when she was slow to understand, he pulled out the police auxiliary card that came with the cloth, stamped by his new paymasters: the new German authorities.

'As good as drafted! Again, my son!'

His mother wrung her hands and scolded, when he came into the house and held the new card out to her.

'Have you learned nothing, my child?'

His grandfather shook his head, refusing to listen, refusing even to look at him, while Mykola told of the wages he'd be earning them.

'For the rebuilding. And winter fodder. I'll be paid in Reichsmarks for the seed we'll need in springtime.'

All their seed stock had gone up in flames, along with their hayricks and the village buildings. But still Grandfather would hear none of it.

'Better you had gone to the partisans.'

He would sooner Myko had gone to the marshes, even if it meant living like an outlaw – and fighting again, like a soldier.

'You'd be fighting for us, at least. Not for Germans. They are foreigners, boy, and they tell us – us! – how we should and shouldn't live.'

Myko's mother and sister were quieter, but just as insistent: 'Tell them to keep their Reichsmarks.'

'And their ration cards.'

'Yes, so we can keep you here.'

'Do that for us, please, Mykola.'

On and on it went. Until Yasia's father told them all bluntly: 'My harvest this year will not feed both our families.' Their families weren't even joined yet, need he remind them? 'You want your boy to marry my daughter?'

He was loud too, not just curt, asking Myko's grandfa-ther: 'How can I give my child to someone who can't keep her?'

And then there were so many tears shed that evening, Yasia doesn't like to remember.

On her lap, the child twists against her, and Yasia hears the same low rumbling talk is still going on around her.

'The partisans will see them off.'

'You think so? And when, though? I don't see any outlaws here this morning.'

'No, I won't go out there.'

'Me either. Not until the yids are gone – and all the soldiers.'

Then Osip stands up.

'Damn the Germans.'

'Damn the Germans,' he says it another time, raising his voice to be heard – and the girl on Yasia's lap sets to crying in earnest.

Osip signals to her: give the child back to its mother, he has heard enough here: 'I have work to get on with. Don't we all have work to do this morning?'

The timber man nods, taking his cue, getting to his feet while Yasia rises.

'Are you going out there?'

'You can't be! What are you thinking?'

'He can't be thinking straight.'

The neighbours call out in scorn and concern as Osip takes his leave of them, and Yasia lifts the baby. Passed hand to hand, the child cries all the louder, but Yasia is glad to be leaving – and to have the size of Osip beside her as she turns her back on his calling neighbours.

'You just watch yourselves. Careful.'

'Better watch out the Germans don't take you.'

Ephraim's back aches from all the standing, but he cannot move to ease it. His shoulders, always so stooped over his workbench, over the frames and lenses, are stiff and painful, and yet the guards still watch them so closely, he can do little more than shift his weight from one foot to the other. But he has Rosa's small hand in his hand, and this is something. This is something.

He knows Miryam will have told the girl to hold it – she will have seen the pain he is in – but still he is glad of his daughter's touch. He and Miryam have been hand in hand like this with their young daughter a good hour now, he thinks, although he has stopped looking at the time; he has tried to stop himself thinking about it.

Yankel will come. He will see sense. Ephraim tells himself this to ease his aches. *He will bring Momik with him.* One suitcase of belongings, winter clothing, food for three days' travel, just as they did this morning.

Miryam laid out their clothes last night. Three shirts for him, three dresses for her.

'We can wear them one over the other, Ephraim; you will see.'

Friends and neighbours had passed on advice, word of mouth: *Take enough for the winter; we must see ourselves through the worst months.* They'd worked out ways to carry more than the allowance, wearing extra layers, sewing rings into hems, and savings into linings; and they'd made lists of items to take, valued weight for weight. *You must bring any tools of your trade.* There was so much practical sense in what they said; Ephraim had even found it comforting, in its own way, this wisdom in adversity.

So he'd packed up his optician's tools, salvaged from his small practice rooms – careful, as he always was. And he'd called Yankel to him: his eldest, and the most puzzling of his children. A worry, always; such a cause of worry for him.

The boy came while Ephraim sat wrapping his pliers, his screwdrivers and his callipers for the journey. Yankel came to stand just inside the door as he was packing his briefcase, so Ephraim had to talk half to his tools, half over his shoulder, as he stooped over his workbench to select the best of his lenses, and the best soft leather to protect them. And he could feel his son becoming quickly restive behind him, eyes and fingers restless, the way he always is. Such a fine-fingered, fine-featured boy, so like his mother with his brown curls and paleness – but without her stillness; Yankel can never stand and listen for any length of time without shifting.

All the same, Ephraim began talking. Telling him how their friends and neighbours had been planning for their resettlement; and how their forefathers had started anew with far less, over and over, down the centuries.

'It seems this is our burden,' he said, slow and careful, because he didn't understand it himself; Ephraim hadn't yet reconciled himself. But when he glanced at Yankel – uncomfortable with being spoken to so seriously, and perhaps just as uncomfortable with the harsh truths he was being told this evening – Ephraim felt himself soften towards his puzzling child. The boy must find it so bewildering, after all, this packing up and leaving, and being told that this is how it's always been. So Ephraim sighed: 'How I would it were different, my boy.'

There was a hush then between them, a few seconds of something like understanding, as Ephraim fastened his briefcase buckles. And because he felt Yankel listening – the boy was really listening, for once – Ephraim spoke to him from the heart that evening; about how much it perplexed him, this sore and cruel history of their people; and how he'd far rather they'd been spared this, at least for another generation.

'You do know, my child, the Germans are only the latest to demand this.'

They'd had the same from the priests and the nobles; the same going back into time immemorial.

'So we will endure it.'

Ephraim said they would line up with dignity when the time came, and then put down his tools and turned to face his eldest.

'We have to,' he told him. 'So we will be able. Do you see now?'

But if he did, Yankel didn't show it.

His eyes, that had seemed to be attentive, that had seemed to be so interested only moments before, closing suddenly over, turning hurriedly inward, as soon as Ephraim turned his gaze on his son.

Ephraim saw Yankel's full-lipped paleness and the boyish jut of his jaw, he saw the stubbornness of all his son's thirteen years – but not what he was thinking, not any longer.

So beautiful, that young face of his, but so hard to read. The boy was so hard to reach; even on those rare occasions, like that evening, when Ephraim tried his best to open his heart to his son.

The schoolmaster said much the same about him. *I am never sure, never quite certain, if Yankel believes schoolmasters are worth his attention;* he wore the same closed expression, displayed the same restless wish to be elsewhere, outside, anywhere but the classroom, and the teacher took it all with his quiet good humour. *He'll listen, your son, but only for so long, Ephraim. There will only ever be so much I can teach him.*

Yankel's school reports were never as good as Ephraim's own had been; nor were they as good as Rosa's, who started school three years after, but quickly caught him up. The boy learned to read just as fast, and his fingers were just as fine as hers. But not his penmanship, or his thinking. His books were blotted and streaked and smeary; he thought in rash and bold strokes, and only ever in short bursts, it seemed to Ephraim, who saw how quickly his eldest grew distracted by daydreams during prayers, or the singing of the Torah – even over mealtimes at their family table. He assumed his son was much the same when seated at lessons.

When the long school morning is over, that's when the best hours of Yankel's day come: this was the schoolmaster's verdict.

His eldest went to the river instead of doing his home-work, Ephraim knew this. Yankel copied down the other boys' answers – or even Rosa's – hunkered on the town-hall steps; Ephraim heard all about it from his customers, and from the other shopkeepers in his small row. In the warm months, when the waters were full and slow, they'd tell him how they'd seen his Yankel wading in the shallows, following the trout shoals. Or crouching in the long grass on the banks, in amongst the insect crawl and hum, whittling at sticks he'd found there, spending hours at little carvings with his clasp knife.

If it were all such harmless pastimes, Ephraim wouldn't have minded – or not so much. But Yankel also joined in with all the working boys when they took it upon themselves to jump from the town bridge into the waters. For the town boys this was a badge of honour, for the farmhands a chance to wash themselves on market days, and Ephraim was uncomfortable with his son's wish to emulate. His boy's body was slender, more sinew and bone than brawn, not built for the hard knocks that working boys seemed to thrive on. But would Yankel listen to him? Yankel would never be told. The boy would nod, as though he'd heard – and then do whatever he wanted.

When the river was frozen, Yankel would slide out on his boot-soles, on a working boy's wager, arms out for balance, jutting out at all angles, and a trail of the younger children following behind him onto the ice, once he'd tested it for them. Each winter, Yankel wanted to be the first to dare; always first and furthest, but never in his schoolwork.

When there was ripe fruit to climb for, he strode out to the orchards. Yankel slept out in barns, or under the stars when the nights got warm enough – or even when they weren't yet – returning home unwashed and coughing, with barked shins and bruises, and boughs of fruit wood for carving. His mother enforced bed rest and poultices, and she fussed and she scolded. But Miryam could never stop him.

Three summers in a row, Yankel was brought home by one or another irate orchard worker; or made to pick for an afternoon in lieu of fruit he'd stolen, fruit branches he'd broken. He limped home from those afternoons exhausted, with fruit-stained shirt and fingers, but the will Yankel was born with seemed to come with vigour to match it, and those afternoons of labouring never served to rein him in.

He ranged all over – with Momik in tow, as soon as Momik was old enough. And Miryam allowed this. Miryam indulged it.

Ephraim's wife is younger; her own youth not so long ago, she still understands its headstrong nature. But there is more to it than that, he thinks: Miryam allows their sons far more leeway than she does their Rosa, giving in to Yankel's stubbornness, just as her own mother always gave way to her self-willed eldest.

And this is the nub of it.

Miryam's wayward brother left for Odessa when she was still a young girl, and then he left the country entirely, sailing for Palestine not long before Ephraim married her. Ephraim hardly knew Jaakov, only that he struck out on his own path. And that Miryam loved him for it, almost as much as she missed him.

So however much she fusses over Yankel's coughs and his bruises, she also takes quiet delight in his adventures. And in how much their oldest dotes on their youngest son. *Lucky to have such a brother; they are lucky to have one another.*

As soon as Momik was walking, Yankel took him every-where, and if the little one got tired, Miryam didn't mind. She said Yankel carried him, easy; she'd seen how he pulled Momik onto his shoulders and kicked stones down the road ahead of them to entertain him. *Better to carry him than leave him trailing.*

True as that may be, Ephraim could never rest with the thought of what their oldest did in those hours, of what risks he took with their youngest.

Once the cherries were dark enough, Yankel would lift Momik into the branches, and climb up after him. And Yankel was wise enough by then to the farmers, so if anyone came after them, he knew the best paths to run, and ditches or thickets to crouch in until they'd gone again; *no need to be frightened.* That's what he told Momik, most probably. It's what he told Miryam, whose misplaced trust was boundless. *Don't worry so: he'll grow out of it.*

In the meantime, the child is incapable of following orders. Ephraim knows it would be just like Yankel to hole up some-where, not line up for the Germans – and it would be just like him to take Momik. Most likely he told his brother that the Germans would never find them: the schoolmaster had carried on teaching them, after all, and the Germans never found out about that.

After the school was closed, the master gave lessons in his parlour. Just to Yankel and Rosa and a handful of others, within the short hours the new laws allowed them. The new laws meant they had to hurry home again afterwards.

'Swiftly, yes?' Ephraim reminded them before they left each morning. 'No dawdling and talking. No forgetting your armbands. And no stopping at the riverbank and whittling either.'

He knew that Yankel still worked at sticks and branches instead of his homework, and that he waded in shoeless under the shade of the town bridge, where he thought he couldn't be spotted by his elders – the schoolmaster had passed on this much.

The farm boys gathered there in the summer when the Communists fled, and the Germans were overrunning the country; they crowded on the riverbank and told each other tales of the fighting, and of partisan hideouts. There were so many rumours at that time of marsh strongholds and brave marsh fighters – Ukrainians who would avenge them, and return the land to its own people – Yankel carved an entire orchard for Momik to play with while crouched in the shade beside those waters, listening to those tall stories. Ephraim thought he may even have heard more of them in the schoolmaster's parlour; he wouldn't put it past the old man to have hope in such fantasies. So, after the Germans brought in their new laws, he was careful to impress on Yankel the need to heed them.

'You do understand, my boy, that we cannot afford to just ignore them.'

It was not right that they had to bow to such unfairness; Ephraim did not want Yankel thinking it was just. But he did want him to see the necessity.

And the boy did see how things had changed for them, because he minded Ephraim's instruction at first, pulling Rosa home in good time – even telling Momik he was to stay inside the house.

Except some of those September afternoons were as hot as

any in June, and the water so tempting. Even to Rosa – who confessed all to her mother, but only after the fact, when it was all too late.

It turned out that Yankel had his sister keep watch by their shoes on the bank, just to be safe, and she told her mother how no patrols ever came their way, so she took to reading instead of watching; Rosa took to daydreaming. She even tied up her dress once to join Yankel in the water.

But the current caught at her skirts, and then Rosa got frightened: if Miryam saw the wet hems, or worse, if Ephraim saw the splashes; *you know how Papa is.*

She told her mother how she tugged at the knots, hauling at the cloth, pulling her skirts higher, retying, but the water was stronger. It pulled them sodden against her legs, leaving them clinging there. And Ephraim knew his daughter as well as she knew him: by the time Yankel turned and saw her, she would have been pink with tears in the summer-slow waters.

But even so, even so, they were still inside the curfew; Ephraim thought they could have hurried home, even then – barefoot if need be.

Except townsmen had stopped to watch them. And others had begun joining them: leaning on the mossy bridge walls, looking downwards, to see who was below there. They were pointing at Rosa in her wet skirts and armband, and they were jeering. Grinning over the Jew girl. Miryam didn't have to say it out loud, Ephraim understood how such townsmen were.

But Yankel saw no danger.

Yankel threw stones at them.

Instead of turning home, as he ought, with his sister in tow, his son threw stones at the offenders. He stood in the shallows, hurling pebbles and his half-finished carvings – curses as well – until the townsmen ducked and fled. They flung oaths over their shoulders in return, but Yankel didn't care.

'Why should I?' He told Ephraim this, defiant.

So surprising, to hear his quiet son speak so loudly. To see Yankel flush too, taking stubborn pride in it, his own thoughtlessness. It gives Ephraim a sharp stab to remember – that the child couldn't see what he'd done. No sense of his own fragility, of the narrowness of those dear shoulders – or of the risk he posed to all of them. Even when the patrol called at their house for days afterwards.

Ephraim had to stand in the street each morning with the soldiers, and account for all their whereabouts. He kept Yankel inside the house at all times – he was taking no more chances. But the boy also had to overhear his daily repentance: 'It will not happen again, you have my assurance, *meine Herren.*'

Ephraim knew to appease them. But it was a daily abasement, a humiliation, and it was too hard to look at his son's face after he was sent back inside, Ephraim kept his eyes averted.

Yankel, in any case, kept his eyes on his schoolwork.

Ephraim insisted he learn his lessons now in earnest, and as he was forbidden to open his workshop, he spent his days sitting with Yankel instead, to ensure the boy stayed bent for long enough over his books.

'Learning weighs nothing,' he told him, over and over. 'Lessons you can carry with you. Don't you see it's our learning, it is our knowledge that has carried us, all through the centuries?'

Yankel did all the tasks the schoolmaster set him. But he would not look Ephraim in the eye any longer.

Ephraim feels that same stab again.

And then he thinks of those two empty beds he found, in the small hours of this morning.

He had not slept a wink – who could sleep with such a day before them? – and still he had not heard them leaving. Rosa had cried and Miryam had brought her to lie in the bed between them; she would only quieten with Ephraim's arms around her, so this is how he lay, all that short and awful night, while Miryam walked from room to room, folding and sorting, repacking their bags, just as unable to rest. She was taking leave, Ephraim thought, and again and again, he heard her tread on the stairs, across the floorboards, in the rooms below him and Rosa. But sleep must have taken even her in the end; perhaps it even took him for a while. Because there was quiet, Ephraim remembers, a strange kind of stillness – a torpor, that came over the house, even over the street outside it – and from which he was only roused by the neighbours' door slamming shut as they left for the factory.

He found Miryam downstairs, chin on her chest, in one of the tall chairs at the back of the kitchen, and it hurts him most to think of this. How startled she was to be woken, finding his hand on her arm – and how her hands flew up to cover her face when he told her that their boys were gone.

He should have known Yankel would do this, he should have been listening; Ephraim thinks he could have stopped them.

But now the whispers start again. Hushed murmurs passing through the crowd around him.

Some in here have come as instructed, others have been brought under duress, but they have all been kept standing and waiting for so long now, they cannot help but whisper, cannot help but worry what might await them.

Transport. Resettlement.

'More of this same treatment.'

Time and fear have given rise to many rumours, passing through the crowd and then back again.

'There are ghettos in Lviv and in Minsk.'

'Yes, and in Poland.'

'Didn't I say so? Didn't I say it's a ghetto they have planned for us?'

'Yes, three days' travel, remember? They told us.'

All around Ephraim, people try to find comfort in this ghetto prospect.

'So it will be Łodz, maybe?'

'You think?'

'Or Warsaw, or Warsaw.'

These names are familiar enough to offer some assurance.

'In Łodz and Warsaw there are many of us.'

There is consolation in the idea of such numbers. But some are still anxious: 'A ghetto is a ghetto. Even with many inside it.'

'Oh, even worse, then: can you imagine? There will be so many of us arriving.'

And then a man nearby contests: 'Will it be a ghetto, really? I heard otherwise. I heard it is a camp we'll be taken to.'

This sets off a flurry of rushed denials.

'It's not a camp.'

'It is not a camp, no.'

'It can't be.'

The whispers are flustered, disconcerted.

'Better a ghetto than a camp.'

'Better a ghetto.'

'Yes, far better. And with our own kind.'

Then the man interjects: 'Enough talk. Enough of this mewling. I've heard enough of it.'

Ephraim's back hurts, his shoulders, so much standing is painful. His insides hurt just as much now from all the worrying, from all this waiting that weighs so heavy on all of them.

But he keeps listening all the same now; he cannot help himself.

And he finds himself listening out for this interjecting man especially, who objects to the mewling, as he calls the worries and the whispers. Ephraim knows that were he to turn and look, it would bring trouble from the guards, but the man's voice is so much louder than the rest, coming from somewhere near the centre of the room, Ephraim has to fight the urge to turn and face him, fight the curiosity, because the man starts interrupting more often. The man starts making corrections, too.

A woman assures her children: 'Soon we'll be driven away.'

But the man puts her straight: 'Soon we'll be driven onto trains.'

He speaks with such blunt assurance, Ephraim sees people all around begin to blink at one another: perhaps this loud man knows more and better, after all?

Ephraim wonders about the guards: are they listening? They must hear all of this, if he can.

He turns his head, just a little, not too much, but the people in front of him have shifted as they whispered, and still more have been pressed in to join them, so he cannot see the policemen any longer. Still, he thinks: all this nervous speculation, the policemen could put an end to it. *They could just tell us when and where we will be taken, if they know. If they had a mind to.*

'We'll be assigned jobs there,' someone insists, still persisting, still preferring the ghetto rumour.

But the interrupting man scoffs: 'You want jobs now? In a ghetto?' He even laughs a little – 'No. Oh no, no' – as though the very idea is risible.

Ephraim sees how people in the crowd try to ignore him; they turn away from his voice again, and continue with their whispers.

'We will be put to work.'

'Yes, that's what I have heard.'

'Yes, they will take us to Poland and make us work.'

But the man in the centre responds: 'They will take us to Poland and make us into soap.'

This last produces such hisses, such intakes of breath. Heads turn back to him, all over the room: a sudden ripple of movement. Arms are raised as people turn to face the man in shock and accusation, lifting their palms in dismay, despite the guards, despite themselves.

'Quiet over there!'

The guards shout them down again; they pound at the metal doors even louder.

'Quiet, now! How many more times?'

But even after the guards have stopped their pounding, and the painful ringing in his ears has subsided, Ephraim still feels the anger in the crowd around him.

He hears people hard by, muttering:

'How can he say that?'

'How can he talk that way?'

They cannot keep quiet now; they must speak their shock to one another, as soon as they feel it is safe enough to do so.

'He should hold his mouth.'

'You should hold your mouth, sir.'

'There are women and children here.'

One woman, her son pressed to her side, is bold enough to turn on him. 'Shame on you,' she hisses. 'Scaremonger.'

But the man is unrepentant. And he will not keep quiet either.

'Should I not say?' he declaims. 'Why should I not say what we all know to be the case?'

He is certain, and he is loud. And then he is met – they all are – with another and even louder barrage from the doorway.

'Silence here, you filthy Jews!'

Ephraim is left with the ringing that follows it, and the ache, too, in his back and shoulders. He is left to wonder who is right here.

Was he right to bring his wife and daughter? Or was Yankel the wiser, defying the order, keeping beyond these four walls?

Ephraim glances at Miryam, at Rosa, as soon as the pain allows this. His girl is leaning against her mother, and her eyes are blank and closing, as though she was woken by the guards but is now almost back dozing. Ephraim thinks: at least his daughter will not have heard the argument; at least she will not have felt all the fear that was unleashed there. He must worry, but she won't have to.

Miryam sees him looking. They exchange the briefest of nods, quiet looks; understanding.

You heard him? Ephraim mouths. And then he mutters. 'How can the man say such things?'

He still finds the thought too appalling; this whole day and all this waiting. All these rumours.

'How does it help us to hear that? To imagine the grave awaits us?'

And then, a little quieter: 'I ask you.'

And after that comes silence.

In the quiet of Osip's workshop, Yasia cuts an apple into quarters, paring away the core, feeding it to the horse, leaning against his warmth in the stall.

Her mother's sacks are stowed now, and Yasia is alone again. Around her stand Osip's workbenches, scattered with curled wood shavings and half-finished joinery: a cabinet, minus half its shelving; a cart brought here for mending, propped against the far wall, listing on its axle. 'I have so much work to do,' Osip sighed before he left her here.

Yasia watched him go – he and the timber man, setting out into the yard with a pair of joists shouldered between them. Osip told her he had to make use of the short working day the Germans have allowed them; the few hours before dark were all he had to make his deliveries. But he said for her to stay put.

'By tonight, please God, the soldiers will all be gone again. And all the Jews with them.'

Osip called it an ugly business, and he warned her to stay clear of it.

'You can sell your apples tomorrow, child,' he told her, letting the gate fall shut behind him.

But she hasn't come here for that. Or not only. Yasia wants to see Mykola.

She hardly slept last night, leaving well before her father woke, with just her mother to see her off. Yasia knows her papa will have raged when she wasn't there to feed and dress her brothers; that he may still be sore at her when she returns, and she doesn't want to have risked that for nothing. So she arranges the fruit in the basket – stalk up, bruises down – just as her mother taught her, and then she hooks the handle over her arm, ignoring Osip's counsel, stowing the knife in her apron pocket. She does everything just as she would on market days, and tells herself: if any soldiers pass her, they'll hardly look twice at a girl come to trade here.

Still, she walks the long way round to be safer, making her way through the alleyways, as best as she can, to the shop-lined market street, stopping by the water trough – one of her mama's familiar spots. Thinking just to linger here a short while, Yasia slices the browning faces off an apple quarter to reveal the pale flesh better, and then she places the cut fruit, clean and pleasing, in the centre of the basket. But no one comes to buy from her.

No patrols pass, but there are no customers either, and the few shop owners who have opened peer at Yasia through their windows, before withdrawing. What is a farm girl doing alone here – and today of all days? Yasia feels their questioning glances; she is uncertain herself now.

She never told her mama – or not out loud – that she wanted to seek Myko out. But she knew her mother understood; Yasia thought her mama even approved. Why else did she not send a brother or two for company? Why else did her mama rise early to plait Yasia's hair for her?

Her mama wove the two long twists around her forehead, as she always did on feast days, pinching her cheeks in the glass so they would look rosy, as much as to say Yasia should pinch her cheeks, look her best and most beautiful, before she sets out to find Mykola.

And the thought of seeing him has the heat in her cheeks rising, it gives Yasia a sharp tug, deep inside her. But it is so many weeks since she saw him, even longer since they spoke to one another. The last time was that drunken evening, so full of arguing, when Myko sat between her father and his grandfather at the table, and her mama wept because of all the shouting.

That was when her papa talked of Yasia not being allowed to marry any longer.

'There will be no wedding, I warn you, until the boy can feed and clothe a family.'

'Don't say that! Why must you say that?'

'I'm only saying it because it's true. Who in their right mind promises his daughter into poverty? We've lived a poor life long enough, I tell you.'

'And so that is what you think of us?' Myko's grandfather stood up at the table. 'You think my boy is not fit to be your son-in-law?'

Yasia had never seen him so angry.

'Mykola will be ten times the man you are, ten times the husband,' Grandfather insisted. 'I see the way you bow and scrape to invaders! You shame your wife there, and your daughter. You bring shame on all of us. Who says I want to see my grandson married into a family like yours?'

But Yasia's father would hear no such insults, not under his own roof.

'Who is bowing?' he demanded. He saw no one scraping before the Germans. 'Look around you. All I see is that my land is mine again. I see new barns and houses, and new roads being laid here. Everywhere, the Germans are building. And we can farm now, just as we want to. That's all I know.'

Yasia's papa turned to Myko, sitting beside him at the table, telling him there was no shame in what he was doing.

'You earn your Reichsmarks. You wear that armband. You're paying your family's way, boy.'

But that had Grandfather white-lipped and raging, and Mykola's mother leaning into her handkerchief and crying; and Yasia wretched as they did all their crying and raging over him.

It was only Mykola who did no shouting that evening; he said so little, it scared her.

But he still came for her later. He saved all his talk for when it was just the two of them in the orchard grass.

Myko sat down close beside her, on the night-cool ground

79

beneath the branches, and he was still quiet at first, still drunk as well, his eyes a little bleary. But he did not put his hands inside her dress: he spoke to her instead.

'Just listen, please,' he said, low and insistent. 'No crying, no shouting. You promise, yes?' And then, when she didn't answer: 'No arguing like your papa. Like my grandfather. Those two old fools. What do they know? I can't listen any longer.'

Myko knew he'd shocked her, talking like that, even if he said it all softly. But he offered no apology, he only leaned his head closer, turning so he could look at her, and his face was so close to hers then, almost touching, and his eyes were still swimming a little, in and out of focus, but when he fixed them on her, they were strange and bright and urgent.

'Your papa thinks all is well now, just because things are going well for him. And my grandfather. My grandfather,' Myko paused and squinted, as though wincing about the old man. 'He thinks pride can replace the roof beams, maybe. Pride can fill the seed stores and the bowls on the table.'

Myko shook his head over the pair of them, each as wrong as the other. And then he shrugged and waved a hand, as though brushing them aside, away into the night air.

'They can shout all they like.' He smiled.

Strange to hear him drunken and brushing off their elders; strange to watch him smile and shrug, and yet still be so serious.

'Who has time for old men and their arguments?' he asked. 'Not me. Not *us*.'

Myko pulled Yasia into his lap as he said this, pressing his forehead to her own one. And he told her he couldn't be waiting until the old men had sorted out their differences.

'I can't just be sitting by now. You understand that, don't you?'

Yasia couldn't answer. She wasn't sure about this; she didn't know if she could ever be sure about anything with the Germans here. But she thought Myko understood that, because he looked at her so intently while he was waiting – and then he just smiled at her anyway, his face close and warm, breath mingling with her own. He told her: 'You'll see. In time, you'll see it too. I know you will.'

Myko was certain. Yasia felt it in the way he held her, and in the way he leaned in to tell her: 'We had the Soviets, remember? Well, now we have new masters. And your father, he might think well of them. But it will be just the same – just the same – under this new lot, I am telling you.'

He said he'd learned that much this past year.

'First they will make their promises. But it won't be too long before they break them all. That's how it works, believe me. No one takes a land out of kindness. Just to take what they can, see?'

Myko kept her eyes on her, all the while he was talking, as though he wanted to be certain she was following.

'You are listening to me?'

He had no need to ask. It was more words than Myko had spoken in all the weeks since his return, and Yasia listened to everything he told her. Because he held her so close to him. And because they had lain here so many nights too, as husbands and wives do, since he came back from being a soldier.

Yasia was still mindful of the evening's argument: how can Mykola marry her if he has no means to keep a family? But she saw too that he'd learned far more while he was gone from them than either of their families were aware of. He was taken away a boy and had come back thinking like this; perhaps he knew more and better than all of them.

And though Myko did not speak of marriage that night in the orchard, not in so many words, he sat with his face close to hers, and he said: 'I've seen how it works, Yasia. The Germans are bastards; occupiers always are. But they will go again – they can only last for so long.' Hadn't they seen that with the Russians? And wasn't everyone glad to see the back of them?

Myko told her: 'The Germans are only here to take what they can get, so the way I see it, we don't have to trust in their promises, do we? We just have to live to see them gone again.'

He'd managed that before, Yasia thought: he'd braved the Germans when he cut his losses and ran from the Red Army, and then he'd walked back through all they'd burned and broken. Myko had seen more harm than anyone she knew, and he'd come back alive to her.

But still it was hard to hear him talk this way. Hard not to shout too, when Mykola told her he'd be leaving for the town as soon as possible: 'I need to start earning.'

Yasia had to bite her tongue all the while he spoke to her, because she thought of the ring, not yet on her finger, and she knew she'd have to bide her time and wait still: Myko would be staying in the new police barracks for the winter, and even beyond that.

'The SS will get townsmen clearing the ground for it,' he told her. 'Soon enough it will be built and ready.'

That meant, soon enough, he would no longer sit at her family table. Yasia could have cried out at the unfairness.

'But it won't be like this always,' Myko promised, keeping on with his talk and with his soothing. 'Just for as long as is needed.' Just until they could farm again.

He would not go east where there was fighting; Myko swore he would never go back to doing a soldier's job. He'd patrol the town streets mostly, or in villages, and most of the auxiliaries were village boys, so he'd be with Ukrainians just the same as him giving the orders.

'There are other police here, too, from Germany,' he told her, so there might be times – now and again – when it would be them he'd have to answer to.

It was this last part that gave him pause. Because he sat back against the straw after he'd told her – but not as though he'd finished with his talking; more like this had set off a whole new train of thought. Perhaps he was thinking of his grandfather: what the old man had said about bowing and scraping to invaders. Yasia wondered if Myko saw shame there, even if her father said there was nothing to be ashamed of.

It seemed to her that so much was different now, not just Mykola. And it was so much more difficult to find a way through. What could she do but wait, while he thought it out for himself?

'I don't have to like it,' Myko said finally. Matter-of-fact, conclusive.

And then Yasia thought she wouldn't have to either. She didn't have to like any of this. It made her feel a little easier.

The police barracks are at the edge of town where the fields start, and the orchards, and while Yasia has passed it before, on her way out to her uncle's in the marshes, she's always been in the dray-back with her brothers, her mother has always been at the reins when they've made that journey, and Yasia isn't quite sure how to get there through the town streets.

She has to skirt through the lanes and alleys, avoiding patrols as Osip cautioned; missing her mother, and the crowding of her brothers around her. Yasia comes to dead ends a good few times, forced to retrace her steps, weary and irritable too now with hunger; she has had nothing to eat since she left the farm this morning, only one or two of her mother's apples, and she peers at the windows she passes, hoping to happen upon one of the town's richer kitchens, with cooks and larders, where she can trade fruit against something warming. But all the windows are shut-tered still.

Yasia has to stop once entirely, thinking she hears a patrol. She holds still at the corner, unsure she has the right to be here under the curfew. Or of how soldiers might look at her, out on her own as she is. *Why so far from home, girl? The market street is the other way.* But it is only a gang of labourers who pass by: a score of men with picks and adzes, on their way back from a day's digging or levelling, and two police guards following, and this has Yasia thinking they could have been working on the new police quarters, so at least she is nearing the town's far boundary.

The fog lifts a little as she walks on, and before long Yasia sees the factory chimney, the old brick kiln, and she tells herself that soon, soon, she will be at the barracks Mykola stays in.

But when she comes to what she feels must be the turning, she finds she cannot go further. This time her way is blocked by soldiers.

So they haven't left the town yet.

Or taken the Jews, like Osip said they would: all that is still to come.

Wooden barriers have been erected at the corner: two heavy trestles with poles between them. And beyond them are so many men in uniform, she can barely see the road ahead. Grey tunics and darker ones mingling, the soldiers stand about, broad-legged and slouching, on the road to the old brick factory, and not at all as she imagines soldiers should; they look more like farm labourers, the way they stand and smoke and talk, leaning against the house walls, as though they've finished a full day's harvest.

A police guard – four or five men in boots and tunics – are standing at the barriers. Strange to see policemen doing a soldier's job; Yasia doesn't like it, or the crowd of uniforms behind them. There are far too many soldiers between here and the barracks Myko stays in; she cannot go to find him.

She should have stayed put, like Osip said. Yasia thinks

she should hurry back to him: didn't he warn her that the town is full of Germans? And already the daylight is fading.

Yasia looks about herself and finds more soldiers in the grey there, by the gates to the brickyard, and a few more policemen; she sees jeeps parked beside them, and a row of trucks too. But though Yasia looks, she sees no Jews.

She blinks at the high wall of the yard: *are they all inside?* It is an uncomfortable thought. All those people. It hardly seems possible.

'You there!'

Yasia starts.

'You there!'

She flinches a little as she turns. There is a jeep pulling up at the barriers, top open, with two SS men inside it; and a driver too, who stands up behind his steering wheel, calling out to the policemen.

'Make way here!'

His voice is Kievan, he is a Ukrainian, not in SS uniform, but he speaks sharply enough to have the police guards blinking.

'The Sturmbannführer has to come through.'

The Kievan does not turn to her; he talks to the men behind the barriers, giving orders for them to be lifted, but still Yasia shrinks away from him. Best to stay away from this ugliness like Osip told her.

She can try again tomorrow, Yasia tells herself, retreating, basket held like a shield in front of her: Osip says she can stay here, after all, so she can find Mykola once the soldiers have gone again.

But still Yasia keeps her eyes on the SS jeep a moment, and on the policemen too, who run to lift the barriers.

And then, as she turns away, she finds herself wondering if Myko runs like that now for the Germans. If he ran any Jews out of their houses this morning.

Miryam is murmuring to Rosa. The girl is tired, and Miryam whispers stories to soothe her.

All around them, children have been crying these past hours as it got dark again. They can't understand this waiting, even less than their parents can, but Rosa is quiet, her eyelids heavy. She has been listening to her mother a good while, leaning close, face pressed to her mother's chest, arms around her waist, fingers wrapped in the ties of her apron. Miryam has kept Rosa patient, occupied with family stories, with Yiddish fables to comfort and console her, and now the girl is drowsy; Ephraim thinks he listens more than she does.

His wife has been talking of Rosa's and Yankel's younger days, and of her own childhood too. But Miryam tells most of all about her brother: about when Jaakov left, and all the hopes he had.

She does not speak of missing him, Ephraim notices: only of his high hopes, and how he sailed with many others like him. Miryam tells of miles and miles of travelling; to Odessa first, overland, and then by ship to Palestine; tales of sailing the oceans for weeks at a time, and then finally arriving. And all this has Ephraim wondering: does Rosa think that's what they will do now?

He looks at his daughter's face, her eyes clouded as

though already dreaming, her soft lids falling, and then he thinks, perhaps that's what Miryam wants: for their daughter to sleep and dream of leaving, with no need to feel frightened. Her uncle left, after all, and now he's in a better land.

Ephraim remembers.

First his brother-in-law's bright features – such an optimist, always – and then his brother-in-law's absence, and Miryam's sadness. But he recalls her joy, too, when a photograph came of him, after almost a year away.

A photograph! The miracle of it! A true likeness, white rimmed and so life-like: Jaakov in shirtsleeves rolled to the elbow, lean and bearded, squinting in the desert sun. He stood, hands on hips for the camera, before a rocky desert background. This was the barren ground he and others would toil to cultivate, Jaakov explained in his accompanying letter; this was the new-and-old land they'd sought, which would bring forth life and all its fruits as they worked it together for the common good.

Miryam bought a frame for the photo – walnut, expensive, and they were only just married then. But a photograph was such a rare and precious thing, and this photograph especially; she kept it on the small table at her side of their marriage bed.

Ephraim looked at it sometimes, if he was alone in their bedroom. And when he did so, he saw not just the brother-pioneer his wife did, the hope-filled face, but also the sunburned forehead and forearms, and the sun-bleached stretches behind his brother-in-law, parched and rock-strewn into the arid distance. Ephraim saw risk there. Of thirst and exposure, and of disappointment; above all, he saw the risk of failure.

Jaakov's letters were few and far between after that first one: his was now a peasant's life of sun-up to sun-down toiling, with little time for writing. The letters, when they came, spoke of satisfaction, but also of setbacks – far louder of those than of any triumphs, at least to Ephraim's ears. But they kept arriving, now and again, over the years.

Miryam read them out for the children, as soon as the children were old enough. She favoured the hopeful parts, about the trees their young uncle had planted – olive and almond, and date palms – and the wells he and his fellow *kibbutzniks* had sunk to keep them watered: they would have to irrigate the new groves until their roots grew deep into the desert earth, and even after that. In one of Jaakov's letters, he wrote how they'd dug for weeks, twenty, thirty feet down into the rocky sand and subsoil, all by pickaxe and shovel, hauling up the rubble by bucket and rope, hand over hand. They'd carved out the wells by dint of sweat and blister and hard graft, only to find the water table sank lower in the dry years. (*Dry years?* Ephraim fumed inwardly as he listened; what was his brother-in-law thinking? What other years were there out in Palestine but parched ones?) He found himself infuriated, whenever he thought of it. To have gone so far, from home and from family, and all that was known to them. Did they not know this land of peasants and nobles? Had they not endured here for centuries, earning their place among the sod and silt and wheat fields? His young brother-in-law had left all of that, and for what, exactly?

Blistered palms and dry wells – and withered almond groves, presumably.

Jaakov sent no more pictures after that first one; neither of himself nor of his groves, thriving or otherwise, and he often went years without writing news home. But the children liked to have his letters read and reread to them; Miryam saved them for high days and holidays, and she read them like stories; solemn, ceremonious, as though they were fables.

The two boys liked to look at the picture too, Yankel especially. He asked more about Jaakov as he got older, wanting more often to hear the stories of his travels and his olive trees, or even just to see his photo. So Miryam brought it down some evenings for the boy to look at after the younger two were in bed. And though Yankel sat with it quietly, content with his own thoughts, never saying very much, Ephraim saw – not without pain – the admiration in his son's gaze. He began to feel, too, how his eldest's eyes measured him, silently: the narrow walls of his workshop, the fastidious labour in the lenses he ground there, the tiny screws he tightened to hold them in their wire frames. The scope of his life was meagre, seen against his brother-in-law's.

But Ephraim cannot think of this, not now; he does not want to feel this bitterness. He just wants his sons with him here. His boys as well as his wife and daughter, all together in their time of need.

So he looks to the doors, and he prays for his sons to be brought through them; his Yankel and Momik. Without bruises – without cuts and bruises, if at all possible – but delivered to him above all.

'They must be found, they must be found soon.'

He mutters now to Miryam, because there is some consolation in hearing himself say this, even if quietly, so as not to disturb his daughter. Saying it, even if only under his breath, makes it feel more likely.

But his wife says nothing; still Miryam says nothing.

She holds the dozing Rosa to her, and she keeps her eyes on the doors, and this last Ephraim can understand, only too well. But why so tight-lipped?

It starts to bother him, her silence. Not a word has passed her lips about their sons since they have been penned in here. So now Ephraim blinks a while at Miryam: her arms so tight around their daughter, and her mouth so closed about their two boys.

Did she know – did she hope – that Yankel would do this? Hide himself and his young brother in an attempt to foil the Germans? Ephraim looks at her face and then he thinks he does see hope there.

'But how can they stay here?' he asks her, a sharp hiss, despite Rosa's slumbers, despite the guards too and their coshes.

Miryam cannot believe, surely, that it would be better for their boys to hide themselves, from the police and from the Germans.

'They will be alone,' Ephraim tells her. Their boys will be left on their own here when they are taken. 'And what then? What then, when we are gone, Miryam?'

She blinks a little; Ephraim sees how unhappy she is at this prospect. But she does not answer.

Still he gets no answer.

Miryam turns her face so he cannot look at her directly; he cannot see what she is thinking. And she turns Rosa with her, as though to shield her.

'There are others,' Miryam murmurs, finally. 'There will be others; Yankel will find them.' And then: 'We have to think that.'

Ephraim doesn't know what to say to her.

What can he say to such naivety?

In Yankel it is forgivable: he is a child still, and guileless. But Miryam? She is clutching at straws, no more: at the possibility of other Jews left behind here, out to save their own skins, or at the benevolence of townsfolk. Ephraim cannot trust his sons to such uncertainty, to the kindness of strangers.

'Who in this town has been kind to us since the Germans came?' he demands, hoarse and vehement. And then he has to stand in silence; he has to try to calm himself.

Ephraim tells himself: there is only comfort in numbers. He thinks of the Jews in Łodz, in Warsaw. Three days' travel, three more days of this, but when they get there, they can make themselves useful to one another, as they always have. He pulls his briefcase closer; his tools and lenses.

But regardless of how much he assures himself, Yankel and Momik are still not beside him.

Rosa is asleep now, almost; lids closing, she sways against her mother's skirts, her mother's arms no longer enough to hold her upright. Miryam lifts her, taking Rosa's sleeping weight on her shoulder, and though Ephraim can see the girl is too heavy for her to stand long, he is too angry to take Rosa from her for the moment.

He stands beside them for a good while, his stubborn wife, so misguided, his sleeping daughter; Ephraim tries fighting down his anger.

And then, around them, he sees a few people are bending – to ease their backs and legs after the long hours of standing. A few even try crouching, tentative, and the policemen seem to allow this. They turn away, or look over the crouching heads, as though they don't see them.

Some time later, Ephraim sees that the schoolmaster's mother is squatting at Miryam's ankles; she sits on her bundle, and the old woman tugs at Miryam's jacket, motioning for her to share it.

Soon they sit back to back, each leaning on the other; Rosa's sleeping form in Miryam's lap, half-hidden in her skirt-folds where the girl will be warmer. The old woman's hand rests on her son's forearm, and Miryam arranges the schoolmaster's torn coat around him; his waking will be painful, when it comes, so now they reach and tuck and reassure him. Watching his wife's care, Ephraim sees her kindness again.

He feels her glances too, off and on, all the while this is going on; not seeking an apology, not relenting, but simply seeing how he is. If something can be done for him. After a short while, she reaches a foot out to their trunk and edges it towards him.

Sit. You sit now, Miryam motions.

She knows how much his back will be hurting, his shoulders. So Ephraim sits down: what use is it now for them to be angry with each other? They should be kinder, he thinks, and it soothes him to sit beside her. Each of them still quiet, but feeling a little kinder towards one another.

Except he sees, too, how Miryam still watches the door, no less sharp-eyed, no less wary than before. And the mistrust in the way she looks at the policemen.

She doesn't see it as a kindness on their part, this turning of a blind eye.

'They won't take us today. Not today, that's all,' she tells Ephraim, when she sees him watching.

Ephraim nods. He has to. He thinks his stubborn wife is right, most likely; he has to concede that much. The Germans will be looking, after all, it stands to reason, for all of those still hidden. Their boys included.

He turns away, leaning himself forward, there where he sits on their one trunk of belongings, and it eases the ache in his back a little, but does nothing for the ache inside him.

How much longer?

The fog was lifting, Pohl was sure of it. The fog was lifting, only for dark to fall.

Evening is here now, and he is still at the encampment, in his small site office with its desk and lamp and cot bed, its four walls of planed boards.

The first shock has passed, leaving a leaden feeling. All day he has found himself incapable of working, unable to rid himself of this morning. Pohl can think of nothing but leaving, and he has sat down at his desk any number of times to write his reasons.

He wrote in rage first. But what he put on the pages was little more than a tirade. No one would take such ravings seriously; even he, in all his anger, could see that. And then, after he'd redrafted, Pohl hit up against doubt and distrust: who to send this to? He could think of no one he was sure of.

Pohl had to force himself to think clearly, and more cleverly: his request for transfer had to have solid ground to stand on – any accusations he made all the more so. But this was no day to find clarity, or assurance, and page upon page ended in shreds in his wastepaper basket.

Now Pohl stands at his office window, and watches for the labour gangs returning.

They are back later than he expected. Work will have started at dawn, perhaps even earlier, but it is well past six by the time he sees the lamps swaying in the dark out there.

The overseers carry lamps and torches; they walk ahead and behind and either side of the columns of workers. Roughshod and roughly clothed, the labour gangs are peasants, they are toilers, their bodies already bent by work long before they started on these road excavations. But still, Pohl is taken aback by the sight of them this evening.

Most are Ukrainians, from nearby settlements, but there are POWs among them: men of the Steppe, peasant soldiers from the vast plains of Asia, their leathery faces wrapped in rags against the chill, some still in remnants of their Red Army uniforms. Russian or local, they are all drawn and wearied, all under-rested; perhaps they are even under-fed, or is that just the lamplight and shadow play-ing tricks on him? Pohl sees boots that do not fit, wrists protruding thin from jacket sleeves. They work the rubble with bare hands; he sees it in their fingers and palms, and it pains him.

The excavation of this stretch has taken far longer than intended. Closest to the marshes, it has been the most difficult, and now they are working against the weather, with just another week, perhaps another fortnight, to finish the drainage work before the ground starts freezing. Pohl and the foremen have already diverted work gangs from other encampments, to the east and the west; instead of surfacing those stretches, they have doubled the numbers manning the trenches here. But still, wherever they dig, up comes water.

The channels at the roadsides fill with it overnight, or even as the workers are still digging deeper. It seeps in underfoot, and then it rises, rises, until the labourers are ankle-deep in mire and water. But still they work on, because the schedule demands it. Their boots slick, their sleeves and trousers sodden, the men dig further, and then they return to the encampment mud-caked, their clothes mud-stiffened, in the half-light of evening. Or even in darkness, it would seem now.

On whose authority are his labourers made to put in such hours?

Pohl looks for Brodnik among the workers, thinking his foreman will be able to tell him; he's already worked on the new Reich roads at home in Poland, so he knows the company's practices. Brodnik knows the SS, too, and how they operate.

('Do we have to deal with them?' Pohl asked him, as soon as he knew he could speak his mind to the man. 'Must the SS have a hand in everything here?'

'This is how it is done, sir.' Brodnik spat on the ground. 'In my home district, too. There are more of them, they can find more labourers than we can. Believe me: my home town was swarming with those arseholes.')

The man is a find in these times; Pohl has often found himself grateful that Brodnik's German is good enough for cursing. He sees the dim glow of lamps being lit beyond the barrack doorway; the labourers are in their quarters, and Pohl thinks that if Brodnik looks out, he will see the light in his own office window; he will call in to report. And then he can ask him about the work hours. Perhaps he can even tell Brodnik what he saw in the town this morning, because he must tell someone.

But now he is stiff and tired, and the small site office is cold around him. Pohl turns away from his window, from all the squalor and disorder, and the barrack houses squatting wretched in pools of miry water. It is too cold and late to be driving after the shock of today – that awful awakening – so he stokes the stove in the corner and then, heavy limbed, heavy of heart, he sits on his cot to unlace his boots.

The company will see red – Pohl is sure of it – as soon as they read his request to transfer: they will not have queues of engineers willing and qualified to replace him. But worse than this will be the SS reaction. Pohl unbuttons his tunic, thinking he will have to confront the Sturmbannführer; the man will want to know his reasons. And how on earth can he start such a conversation?

Pohl has come to know the SS man in charge here. Sturmbannführer Arnold often stops at the encampments;

not to deliver the labour teams – that is left to his subordinates – but to show the roadworks to visiting officers, or just to put questions about the headway they are making.

'You will forgive my enquiring.'

Pohl does not work under him, and Arnold is mindful of this nicety. They are the same age too, so Pohl thinks he cannot pull that rank, either. They probably went to the same kind of school, even; Arnold is familiar, a little too much so. A fellow provincial grammar-school boy grown older, softer about the middle, receding; more suited to desk work than life in uniform.

'How long now before your labour teams can start on the surfacing?'

Arnold has ambitions for the district, and he always manages to remind Pohl, even if not in so many words, that the road is to serve the Reich and its expansion: delays to its construction will delay all the SS plans to improve the new territories.

But he listens, Arnold. He does listen – and always with interest that seems genuine – to Pohl's elaborations of the building stages, and the construction company's projections. The man has shown himself receptive to Pohl's suggestions; even in their earliest meetings, Pohl quickly got the feeling that Arnold wanted to build the road just as well as he did – albeit for different reasons.

Already they've built the road higher than planned for: the terrain demanded this, and Arnold acceded, allowing Pohl to add layers for drainage, and more layers to lift the surface further above the flood plain. They'd had to divert from the intended route there, too, north of the town boundary, widening the curve it took to avoid the start of the marsh-land – and to avoid the partisans there. All this meant losing at least three of their early weeks to the rerouting, but Arnold had seen the sense in this.

Pohl got the feeling that Arnold saw this road differently from his superiors – differently enough, in any case, to talk a little more openly. If not about how to make this road beautiful, or admirable, as Pohl still felt it could be – a true feat of engineering acumen – then at least to be attentive when Pohl asked – quite bluntly – for a little more forbearance.

'You must understand, Sturmbannführer,' Pohl told him, in one of their frankest exchanges, only a fortnight ago now, walking back to the jeeps after one of Arnold's checking visits. 'The Reichsführer SS must understand too, surely. He hasn't chosen the best terrain to build a road through.'

Arnold looked up at hearing Himmler's rank invoked, Himmler's judgement brought into question. But he did not slow, or show any shock or disapproval; he gave no sign that this idea was news to him. Arnold took Pohl's elbow instead, a friendly gesture, almost paternal, leading him to one side, away from the SS drivers, and Pohl thought he might be advised – one grammar-school alumnus to another – to keep his counsel. *Keep such thoughts to yourself; don't be a fool, man. Don't lay yourself open.* But Arnold simply nodded for him to continue.

'The Reichsführer SS; you were saying?'

Pohl was hesitant at first.

'We are behind, Sturmbannführer, but for good reason. We all wish to see the road completed. But out here, you see, such work cannot be hurried.'

'You think we hurry you unduly?'

'At the expense of quality. Yes, I do.'

Pohl's answer came quickly, and it came out more sharply than he had intended, out of nervousness. But Arnold smiled then. And he nodded again: was that agreement?

Pohl had never gone this far before in venturing his opinions, but now he'd dared, and he was meeting no resistance. So why not go further? If he didn't, then surely no one else here would. Pohl had Arnold's attention. More: he had the feeling of having Arnold's ear, then.

'Go on, Pohl,' the Sturmbannführer told him.

So he did.

'A road is there for such a long time,' Pohl started, still careful. 'A good road, in any case.' One that doesn't flood in the winter, or crack and sag for want of groundwork. 'And without a proper route through here, this district will remain impossible to trade with. Stuck in the Middle Ages.'

Arnold wished for something more than a rough-shod thoroughfare for peasants and petty traders, Pohl knew this. The man wanted the district to be prosperous – and to prosper with it, no doubt. And since this damned Reich of theirs was to endure for such a long time – a millennium, interminable – Pohl told Arnold: 'It takes time and men to build well.'

It really was that simple. They needed either more time or more labourers.

'Hurry alone isn't good enough. Hurry is a false economy.'

Once he'd put it like that, Arnold waved away his driver, urging Pohl to walk on with him.

They discussed the depth of the excavations, the tonnage needed from the quarries to fill the trenches, and the work days left available now the winter was almost upon them.

'The frosts here are hard and long,' Pohl reminded the Sturmbannführer. They would bring excavation to a standstill, and that would delay the surfacing, delay the completion further. They needed more labourers, to redouble their efforts, get the digging finished. 'The ground will be solid; down to three metres, my foreman tells me.'

No spade or pick would break through that, however much Himmler willed it.

Pohl didn't say that last part out loud; he left that moot, to hang in the air between them. But the Sturmbannführer gave a faint smile in response, as though conceding: he knew his leader was liable to hubris.

Arnold said nothing out loud, though, until he'd thought it all over, so Pohl felt some of his nervousness returning as he strode beside him back to the jeeps in silence. Unnecessarily, as it turned out.

'You do your job well, Pohl,' Arnold concluded the interview. 'I will put your case. Be assured.'

Now Pohl looks at the clock: Brodnik still hasn't called in to report, and he has to wonder again at his foreman's tardiness, at the hours he kept the workers in the field today. Pohl has the sense of wrestling with this irregularity as he lies down on the cot, too tired to think about it properly.

Tomorrow, Pohl tells himself as sleep comes to take him, he will talk to Brodnik. And he will talk to Arnold. The man already sees the need for more workers: he will listen to his concerns about the work hours, surely. Perhaps he will even put his case to the road authorities – speed his transfer, so he can leave this place behind him.

But then Pohl thinks again of the schoolhouse: all the soldiers massed outside it, and the old couple shoved onto the paving.

Did the Sturmbannführer order that as well?

4

'You're a brave child. Or foolish.'

In the mayor's kitchens, the housekeeper takes Yasia's apples, one by one, from her basket, looking them over, scolding her for knocking at the windows so early. But she buys all of Yasia's fruit, and she asks for more too.

'You bring them later, girl. When it's properly light outside.'

The woman lines Yasia's basket, with eggs and bread and pancakes; she wraps them in a napkin to keep them warm for her, and she gives her coffee as well, a whole canister, before she sends her on her way again. Last night, Yasia promised Osip she would fetch some, to stop him grumbling about her being gone so long yesterday and slipping back only just before curfew – *What would your father say?* So she is glad to take it, and to be on her way back to his yard.

The fog has gathered again overnight; the mouths of the alleyways are shrouded and the steps slippery underfoot as she leaves the mayor's basement. But it is light enough – just – to be out and walking.

Yasia cuts past the well and the dairy and the drinking trough – all deserted, all grey shapes in the fog. None of the shops on the market street look like they will be opening; few lamps are lit in the houses she passes. Yasia has seen nothing and no one yet this morning, save the mayor's housekeeper – and the three German trucks that came at first light.

They came roaring past Osip's workshop, waking her among the straw bales; Yasia felt them through the floorboards, under her bare soles, as she got up, anxious, from her blankets; and then she just caught their dark forms through the glass, the red blur of their tail lights. Yasia stayed there at the window, until they were gone and even after. And now she thinks about them as she walks, because the trucks were heading north, perhaps to the factory, perhaps to the barrack block, and so she wonders: if they woke Myko when they got there. Or if he was up and dressed already, all set to hear the day's orders.

Yasia frowns a little at the thought. But she has orders of her own to follow this morning. The housekeeper has offered to buy a whole barrel load of apples – so Yasia will have butter and sausage, and three sacks of flour to take home. It will mean coring and slicing, stringing the fruit rings onto cords for drying, and so most of the day will have to be spent in working. But the woman has offered her a meal too, when the work is done with.

'The soldiers will be gone by that time – please God,' the woman told her. 'So if you bring a pot, you can take a hot meal back to whoever you're staying with.'

If she worked fast enough, Yasia decided, she could take that pot to Mykola.

So now she hurries back to Osip's, thinking to lay out his breakfast and then get back to the mayor's kitchens; she can haul the apples there in Osip's hand cart, she won't even have to wake him.

It is getting lighter, but the lanes are still deserted, and the coffee pot clanks now and again at her thigh as she keeps up her stride, loud in the quiet. Wary of more trucks arriving, she takes a winding path through the side streets; Yasia cuts down one shuttered lane and then another, all empty and echoing, before she sees she is not alone out here.

At the next turning, she sees two sets of narrow shoulders: two figures in the mist ahead.

One taller, one far smaller, they look to her like children. Winter caps pulled low about their ears, they have their backs to her, walking swiftly, almost at a trot, almost the full length of the lane between them. Yasia glimpses them just before they turn the corner: an older boy, a step ahead, and a younger one holding tight to his jerkin, pulled along behind him. Then they are gone again.

They are only boys, not soldiers, so Yasia is not frightened. But who puts their children out at such a time?

Yasia picks up her pace, unwilling to be outside too long herself, and she holds the canister tighter to stop its clanking, to feel its warmth between her fingers. Her thoughts on the working day ahead of her, Yasia's strides grow longer; she makes the turning – and there are the boys again.

The older one must have left the other standing in the shadows by a cellar entrance; Yasia is just in time to see him climbing the steps again. He takes the younger one by the elbow, pressing onwards, moving faster now, and furtive. Did he try the cellar door? Are they stealing? What a thing to risk in a town full of soldiers.

The older one knows she is behind them. Yasia can see from the tilt of his head that he is listening for her step, or for the canister's clanking. He seems keen to keep ahead of her, because he doesn't try another doorway, he keeps on moving, and when his young brother stumbles, he hoists him onto his back, a practised movement.

This boy is slender, his stride a little gangling, but he is fleet like a farm boy, like her brothers, even with the younger one to carry. So Yasia thinks they might not be stealing, they might just be farm children, caught off guard by the empty town streets, just like she was yesterday morning.

She has gained on them, but the fleet boy does not turn to look, and neither does the young one gripped to his shoulders. Yasia thinks the older one must have told him not to: both have that stiff and listening look about them.

Then the older boy steps out abruptly – into the road, across the flagstones, making for the next available turning – and Yasia sees his profile as he crosses: the distrust in his young features. How he turns his face just far enough to see she is no German, and then a little further, catching hold of her eye just long enough to let her know he's seen her.

Yasia drops back enough for them to notice. Farm children or not, she doesn't want them worrying.

But they take the same route as she does, all the same turnings, and she has to stay behind them: she knows no other way. Soon they will be at the town square.

Yasia thinks of the trucks that passed by Osip's workshop just this morning. How they must have driven across the town square on their way north, and she does not like the thought of the boys being anywhere near them. No children should be out here, she tells herself; no town should have to sweat like this under curfew. Yasia mutters inward curses at the soldiers, wishing them gone again, as soon as possible. She finds herself looking out for the boys too, as she reaches the side of the town-hall building.

It doesn't take long before she sees them. They keep to the shadowed edges, the thickest of the fog, but Yasia can just make them out: how the older boy slides the younger one down from his shoulders, taking him by the hand and pulling him further. They don't look her way again, too intent on their purpose, and Yasia cannot decide yet: if they are trying to hide, or what they are doing here. But she sees that they only slow when they get to the schoolhouse.

Is that where they were heading?

The older one could be a schoolboy, but the other is far too young for books and learning.

And then she sees the mess around the schoolhouse entrance. The broken chairs, splintered doorway; is that broken glass across the threshold?

'No!' she hisses. 'Don't!'

Yasia calls out to both of them – too loud in the silence – and the boys pull together, startled, among the splintered school desks.

'You have to stay away from there,' Yasia gestures; she can't help herself ducking along the wall to stop the boys.

The younger one hides behind his brother as she comes to

a halt; she is still a pace or two away, but she feels how the older one glares at her, frightened.

'You shouldn't be out here in the first place,' Yasia tells him, frightened as well now, startled at her own noise. 'Not until the soldiers go.' And then she presses herself back against the stonework.

The schoolhouse porch is dark, and the doorway strangely gaping; Yasia doesn't like to look at it, or to get any closer – it must have been the Germans who did this. The older boy's face is pale, watching her; it stands out sharply against the school wall, and Yasia glances up at the windows, all around the town square. All she sees are shutters and curtains, but people could still be looking through them, and she doesn't want anyone catching sight of her.

'It is not safe here,' she warns, but a little softer: Yasia doesn't want to be overheard either, giving out warnings.

The older boy blinks at her, no longer glaring – not now he sees that she is frightened just like him – and then they both stand a short while, watching each other, guarded: getting the measure of one another.

Yasia sees his eyes are quick, just like his movements, and he is just as young and thin as she'd thought he was from a distance. But it is shoes he and his brother wear, not work boots – and no farm boy wears shoes like that, or breeches either.

These boys are her betters, they must be: Yasia feels this. They are rumpled – not long awake, perhaps – but still neat and clean for all that, the way her brothers are on church days, and never otherwise.

She has caught these two out at something – that much

is certain. Yasia sees how the tall one has a hand on the younger boy, keeping him hidden behind him. He may be a town child, but he knows he's in the wrong here; and he is thirteen, fourteen at most, and narrow with it, so he is no match for her.

'You shouldn't be out,' Yasia repeats, in a whisper, but meeting his eye now, to be sure that he heeds her. She thinks they must have broken the curfew overnight, sleeping rough somewhere they shouldn't have.

'You should be more careful,' Yasia tells him. No one should stand around like this, even in daylight.

But it seems the older one doesn't want to be told off by a farm girl, because he turns his face away, glancing to the schoolhouse doorway, as if readying to pull his brother inside, away from any police patrols – away from her too. So Yasia shakes her head in warning.

'They will come back, the soldiers.' He has to find a better place to hide in.

And then she finds the younger one is watching her.

Dark curls, fine features, small face peering from behind his brother's back; his eyes are just as quick, but without his older brother's sharpness. Yasia sees, too, how his gaze shifts from her face to the bread in her basket.

Their clothes are good, but they are slept in, and how long since the pair of them have eaten?

They haven't moved since she mentioned the soldiers, and Yasia thinks they must be waiting. For her to speak again, maybe, offer them a heel of bread. Or show them the way somewhere.

But she knows of no hiding place. And she has to go too

now: Yasia has wasted too much working time, and she doesn't like being in sight of all these windows.

'You need to go where no soldiers are. That's all,' she tells the older boy bluntly. 'I can't help you.'

His face closes over as soon as he hears this; as though he already knew she'd say that – or he should have guessed as much. He turns away from her, and Yasia lets out her breath: at least she's got them moving.

Then the older boy lifts the younger one, he swings him onto his back again, and when Yasia sees his smallness, she finds herself asking: 'Your house?'

Because the town is small and their home can't be far away. But neither of them answers. They stand before her, and Yasia thinks of Osip's workshop, just along the lane there; the low room above it, under the rafters. How there is room enough for two more among the straw bales; food enough in her basket.

'Hurry now,' she hears herself usher them. 'Just until the soldiers go. No longer.'

Yasia sends them ahead of her along the side of the town square, and she still doesn't like it. But then she doesn't have to, and the boys can move on again, as soon as the soldiers do.

It is late on in the morning when Pohl sees a jeep drive into the encampment.

Mud-spattered and mud-smeared, even the windscreen, the sight of it puzzles him: there are no site visits scheduled, he had been expecting no interruptions. But as he steps out of his office doorway, and the jeep draws up to park by the barrack building, Pohl sees it is an SS man doing the driving, and that Brodnik is in the passenger seat.

'The Sturmbannführer called at your boarding house this morning.'

The driver hails Pohl across the mud as he climbs out of the vehicle: it is one of Arnold's subordinates, with orders to speak to Pohl directly.

'I tracked down your foreman here at the roadworks.' He gestures to Brodnik, getting out of the jeep behind him. 'But there was no sign of you.'

Where has he been all this time?

The question is implicit. It is impertinent too; this SS driver has no authority to be asking. Except Pohl knows Brodnik must be wondering also: why has he not come out for the usual inspection? He can see it in his foreman's face as he walks over to join them: why is he staying here and not at the boarding house?

'I prefer to be out here,' Pohl says. 'I can work out here,' he tells the SS man curtly. 'I am here to see this road is built. And properly.'

He does not like the way the soldier looks at him. Too direct, too certain.

'I have been working on the schedule,' Pohl continues, looking to Brodnik to confirm this. But he does not lie well; Pohl knows this about himself, so he adds: 'Our other encampments are well ahead of us.' Because this is true. 'If we had more labourers on this stretch, we could be working at the same pace; I have said this before to the Sturmbannführer.'

The subordinate hears him out, letting him talk on until he has finished. But then he gives a brief nod – brisk, impatient – as though he didn't need to be told any of this.

'I was sent only to find you, nothing more. You need to speak to the Sturmbannführer directly. So we will go to him now.'

Was that an order? It sounded like one. The soldier is already walking to his jeep: refusal is not something he expects.

'I'll drive ahead,' he tells Pohl. 'You follow. It will be faster.' He says all this over his shoulder.

Pohl had been expecting to walk the usual site route, conduct the usual inspection of works, which this man wouldn't understand in any case. But now it seems he must climb back into his car, most probably return to the town, and Pohl does not want to go there; even less with an SS man.

'Your foreman will drive,' the soldier calls, and Pohl is grateful for that much at least, for Brodnik's company.

But the drive back to the town is interminable.

Pohl has to wait before he can speak freely; Brodnik takes the wheel and updates him on the morning first, in case Arnold asks them: how many labourers are still laid up, and how many are back at work – the damp and cold have led to influenza, not helped by the cheek-by-jowl living quarters.

'In the town yesterday morning,' Pohl starts. 'You should know this before we get there.'

But Brodnik stops him, shaking his head, pointing through the windscreen at the SS man in the car ahead of them.

'He already told me,' he says. And then: 'I know what they do. They did this in my home town too.'

Pohl thinks Brodnik must have seen the same thing he did. The shouting and herding. Are they doing the same thing everywhere they get to? But his foreman is terse, closing down the conversation. 'Better you think now, sir, what the Sturmbannführer wants with us.'

Pohl looks out at the dank and passing landscape, disquieted.

He thinks of his plan last night, to speak to Arnold. *Foolish.* Pohl thinks of the things he wrote yesterday – all those torn and angry pages in his wastepaper basket at the encampment – and he fears he has been reckless.

Even the things he wrote this morning seem dangerous. Neat and carefully phrased, but critical all the same. He took pride, even, in sneering between the lines at the Nazis here. At their ineptitude and over-reaching. *First comes pride, and then the fall.* Pohl imagines the pages falling into Gestapo hands, and his stomach shrinks at this possibility.

Pohl tries telling himself he is small fry: *just an engineer, just a road-builder.* A man of no consequence. The SS and the policemen here in the district, they will have enough on their hands – surely – tracking the partisans in the marshes, and all the people in the villages who shelter and supply them.

They have enough on their hands transporting the Jews away.

Pohl's mind turns back to the pounding on doors, to the old people he saw hurled onto the pavement yesterday morning. The SS are even rounding up the old, who could be of no harm to them.

It does not help him to be reminded.

They are nearing a turning – the last they must pass before they get back to the town again – when Pohl sees headlamps in the grey ahead of them. Two sets: there are two vehicles lurching out of the nearby village, drawing up to the road along which they are driving.

Not jeeps this time: Pohl is grateful not to see more SS officers; no Gestapo either. They are trucks, both of them, and their dark and bulky outlines are just passing the last of the village houses. The rear truck is covered but the other one is open to the elements, and as they draw nearer, Pohl's eyes pass quickly to the shapes in the back of this lead vehicle.

It is a truck full of men; he can make that much out, even through the fog. But they are not Jews, as he first feared – at least Pohl does not think so; he sees no white armbands. They are all dressed in rough clothes such as the peasants here wear for toiling: it looks like a work detail, picked out from among the villages along this back road.

Pohl thinks – Pohl hopes – that the SS have picked up workers, and now they are taking them elsewhere. And then the road curves as they get closer, and his view of both trucks becomes clearer.

The rear one is covered by a tarpaulin, and in the other, all the men are standing. How many? Thirty? Maybe more, even. The men grip the metal frame as their truck lurches; one by one, both trucks turn onto the road ahead of them, and when Pohl sees they are heading for the town as well now, he finds himself thinking: perhaps this is a new labour team for him and Brodnik to take to the encampment. It could be the quarrymen they need to speed up the breaking of stone and the shovelling.

The men are all hunched against the cold, but a work detail seems a reassuring thing; the sight of a potential labour team is welcome after all his anxious brooding. Even if the SS are leading him a merry dance to take delivery.

The trucks are slow on the road ahead of them, so the SS man overtakes, and Brodnik must do the same. And then, for a few long seconds, they drive alongside the lorries, and Pohl can't help but turn to look as they pass them.

The first is empty – just a flapping and dark tarpaulin; in the second, the men stand with shovels. But the kind for digging sod and soil, not rubble.

They are not the quarrymen he was after; perhaps they are not road workers at all.

Pohl watches in his wing mirror as the trucks fall back into the fog, and he sees that some of the men watch him too. Grim-faced, they make a grim sight in the cold.

The landscape and the receding figures are the colour of ashes.

What do the SS want with him?

When they come across the town bridge, Pohl keeps watch on the trucks through the rear windscreen, wary that they seem to be following for so long. But then they slow and peel off behind them. And when Pohl turns to check one last time, after they pass the orchards, he finds them receding; soon he loses sight of them entirely behind the long wall of the factory buildings.

The SS man drives on another minute, two, and then they draw up on rough ground by the new police headquarters.

There are jeeps there, more than Pohl is used to seeing here. Brodnik parks by the SS man, at the end of a long line of vehicles beside the new barrack building.

'What is this about, do you think?' Pohl sits beside his silent foreman, unwilling to get out and start proceedings.

But the SS man motions them to get moving, pointing them beyond the barracks to the older building, stone and solid, that the SS have requisitioned, so he and Brodnik must climb out of the car to follow him.

Inside, they are led through the ground floor, to the wide back office where Arnold is at a table. Papers are spread before the officer, a plate of bread and cheese and apples in the middle of piles of folders, and he signals acknowledgement as Pohl and Brodnik enter, but keeps attending to his paperwork.

Left to stand across the desk from him in silence, Pohl can't help but feel a point is being made here. He kept the Sturmbannführer waiting, now he will have to stand until this is understood; he has to know his place here. Unnerved, Pohl steps over to the window.

Beyond the pane, beyond the barrack boundary, there is a wide stretch of empty ground, cleared within the past week from the rough-churned look of it. It reaches as far as the factory on one side, and the scrubland on the other; the abundant undergrowth that marks the end of the town, and the start of the countryside. The acre or so before him probably looked just like that until recently: Pohl can see all the scrub has been dug out, leaving wet and empty earth and a few root remnants, while at the near edge, there are piles of sand and grit and timber; to make ready for more barracks, perhaps, or other buildings.

No end to what the SS want to build here; there is no end, Pohl thinks, to their need for labourers.

He finds himself wondering: if the SS mean to extend this town further, will they still supply road labour teams, or only look to man their own construction work?

No more work details. Is this what Arnold will tell him now? *We've done all we can for you and your schedule, Pohl.*

But then Arnold calls to him. 'You need more manpower.'

Caught off guard, Pohl turns to find the SS man is standing, waiting.

'I may have the solution,' Arnold announces, and then he points to the open doorway; a loose gesture to somewhere beyond it – perhaps to the factory.

'I have some here for you.'

Brodnik is at his heels, and Pohl can feel the man's misgivings as they follow the Sturmbannführer inside the former brickworks. They stride through one brick passageway and then the next, a brisk procession, passing open doorways, disused offices and storerooms. A few of them are empty, most are peopled with policemen off duty; with soldiers too, sitting and waiting and smoking inside them. *Why so many soldiers here?*

And then they come to a high and guarded doorway that has Pohl uneasy as it is pulled open.

A mass is gathered inside.

A throng of people. So many.

They sit and squat and stand, each pressed against the other, leaning chest to back, cheek to shoulder. Families with children, women, old people, all of them with white armbands between shoulder and elbow; all with trunks and bundles piled beside them.

Lauf, Dreckjuden! Pohl thinks of the SS outside the

schoolhouse and the old couple hounded; his stomach tightens at the memory as he steps inside behind the Sturmbannführer.

A narrow walkway has been left clear at this end of the factory floor; two metres of empty space, marked by a rope that the people are crowded behind. At the far end of this clear space is another doorway. Police guards stand at intervals all along the wall leading to it, but there is just enough room for the Sturmbannführer and his company to pass through, and Pohl wishes the man would get a move on, pass along here swiftly.

But he looks, too, at the Jews – Pohl can't help himself.

His eyes scanning for a frock coat and shawl, the old couple he saw herded, he finds more faces than he can count; not the two he saw yesterday morning, but many old and many young.

Pohl sees women squatting on the floor, their arms around their sleeping children; and that these arms are there to shield them from being trodden – by the people around them, or by the procession he is part of. Pohl sees their shame too, at having to squat like this, at being looked at this way by a group of passing officials. He is ashamed to be caught staring.

Pohl lifts his face, wanting an end to this discomfort, thinking there must be another room beyond this, housing the labourers he is after. But the guards have come to a stop here, so he turns to the Sturmbannführer for explanation.

'I need road workers.' Pohl points at the far doorway. He sees only families in this press before him, people with trunks packed for travelling. Pohl thinks: *All of them have been brought here to be taken elsewhere.*

'Where is the work detail?' He turns to the Sturmbannführer again, still expecting to be led onwards.

'Here, man,' Arnold tells him, short. 'You must select them. You must take whoever you think will be useful.'

And then he points to the assembled townsfolk: shopkeepers and clerks, schoolteachers; respectable and indoor people in suits and spectacles. But there is something in this gesture: it is tight, abrupt; the man does not have his usual dry and careful composure.

'There will be some you can take,' he says. 'There will be. Take now; this is what they are here for.' And then, a little quieter, a little more pointed: 'We have delayed things here, Pohl, so you can choose from among them.'

Pohl looks again to the faces, to the coats and shawls and shoulders, and then he looks to Brodnik. But he still does not move: Pohl still does not see labourers, and perhaps the Sturmbannführer knows this, because he steps forward.

Casting his eyes across the crowd before him, Arnold selects a young man, beckoning him out from behind the others. He has to keep on beckoning, because the young man is nervous.

'Come on, now,' he urges.

The Sturmbannführer summons the young Jew forward, motioning for him to duck under the rope, to stand clear of the rest – and then: 'You see? Here you have a labourer.' He gestures to the young man.

But the boy is not a peasant, not a toiler. He does look like a worker of sorts: his shoulders are broad enough, and his hands work-toughened for one so young. But Pohl does not move to take him.

'Foreman,' Arnold orders, impatient.

He turns away from Pohl, dismissive, motioning for Brodnik to assist him. And then, while Pohl watches, his foreman takes the lead.

'What can you do?' he asks the selected boy, first in Ukrainian and then – with a glance to Pohl – in German, so he can understand him.

The young man speaks in a mutter.

'Wood,' Brodnik translates. 'This boy here is an apprentice. We can use joiners like him to build the next encampment.'

Arnold nods in agreement; Pohl sees him.

And although Pohl has agreed to nothing here – nothing – the foreman takes the SS man's cue instead, continuing with the selection the Sturmbannführer has started, calling out across the assembled heads in German first, then Ukrainian: 'Hold your hand up if you are a joiner. If you can work wood – well enough to build with.'

A few hands are raised in response, broad-palmed, like the young man's.

'Hold your hand up too if you are a quarryman,' Brodnik continues. They need quarrymen most of all, Pohl thinks; if they can find more stonebreakers here, then this might be worthwhile – perhaps. But he does not like this, and he sees no likely candidates; no more palms raised.

'If you're a stonemason, then. A stone-worker of any kind,' Brodnik qualifies, and this yields another two arms.

The foreman looks to Pohl, and then to Arnold: they need more stoneworkers than that, this is clear enough to all of them.

'Bricklaying? Hod-carrying? Who can turn their hand to labouring?' Brodnik spreads the net wider, and then the young man who was first selected raises a hand behind him.

He says something to the foreman, words Pohl can't understand, but he repeats himself, insistent, and then Pohl sees that many in the crowd are listening, intent now. Enough faces are turned to Brodnik that he has to respond to the young man's questions.

He offers curt words, but they set off a flurry of whispers, and these only get louder when the boy calls into the section of crowd he came from. Pohl can't see who he calls to, just that his gestures are urgent: the boy points at Brodnik first and then at Pohl as well, and he keeps calling until the police guards step forward, raising their truncheons.

'What did he say, the boy there? Why was he pointing?' Pohl strides across to his foreman while the guards call for silence. 'What did he ask you?'

'If selection means he can stay here.'

Brodnik looks at him, blunt.

'He was telling them to put their hands up – all his cousins, and the uncle he came with.' His foreman points into the crowd.

More hands have been raised there in the meanwhile, and more faces are turned to Brodnik, waiting for his attention. But many more in the crowd are watchful, eyeing both him and Pohl, mistrustful, holding their bags and bundles close to them.

'So what did you tell him?' Pohl asks. 'Did you tell him how it is?'

Once the barrack house is built, this apprentice will have to break stones like the rest of them, or dig ditches. Or he will go east to the new encampments being marked out beyond here: the labour teams move with the road; some among their workers even came with Brodnik from Poland.

'Did you?' Pohl insists.

But Arnold cuts across his questions: 'Foreman? Foreman, continue please.'

Brodnik can only glance at Pohl in answer before he turns to the crowd again.

'Any labourers,' he calls out. 'We need labourers of all kinds. If you have done farm work before, you put up your hand now.'

Brodnik starts pressing through the crowd, forcing his way through to those who have raised their arms, and Pohl watches as he talks to each man briefly before pushing onwards.

'Keep your hands up so I can see them.'

Some he sends to the front, to where the apprentice is standing, others he leaves where they are – not accustomed to toil, perhaps, or just not strong enough – and Pohl is somewhat reassured by this. Any men Brodnik chooses will have to work outside, long hours, and in all kinds of weather, and his foreman will not choose those who cannot cope with this – surely.

There are seven at the wall now, including the apprentice. Pohl thinks they will have fifteen, perhaps twenty new workers at most, at the rate Brodnik is choosing. They need more than that, but it is plenty enough from among these people.

It would be asking too much of them, and Pohl has already seen more than he wants of this selection. He turns to Arnold to signal this, but the Sturmbannführer shakes his head.

'You can choose more. Choose more, man.' He directs this to Brodnik, turning away from Pohl's signal.

The foreman says nothing, he looks neither to Pohl nor to Arnold, he only continues through the crowd.

Did Brodnik do this in his home town too? Pohl thinks he must have done it somewhere before, this selecting. He cannot read his foreman's expression, but the man knows the form, that much is clear: he is talking to more now, going back to men he passed over; men without their arms raised, even. All with the Sturmbannführer watching.

Brodnik must choose more, and there are scores of men here, it is true. But for all this looking, Pohl still doesn't see workers among them. Not labourers. So many in this crowd are old too; Pohl looks once more for the frock coat, the white head, and sees too many white heads before him.

Pohl steps forward.

'No one older than forty.'

He feels the pulse, beating hard at his throat at speaking out like this; a sharp prickle of sweat across his scalp. But he wants no one chosen who is unfit for labouring; no one unwilling either. So Pohl repeats himself, and louder, to ensure that Brodnik hears him: 'Only young workers; strong workers who know what they are doing.'

He doesn't look at Arnold, Pohl keeps his eyes on the crowd, on those whom Brodnik is choosing, still half looking for the old man, not wanting to believe him in here; or the old woman herded with him.

Would Brodnik select women? The thought gives him pause.

'No women either,' Pohl calls, just to be certain.

He has heard of female labourers used on other roads; female POWs; perhaps they are used in Poland. But Pohl will not have that on any stretch of road he works on.

'No women of any age,' he says, just to have it asserted.

Pohl sees how Brodnik hesitates, looking to Arnold this time for confirmation. But the officer assents: 'No women, then.'

And so Pohl nods, a terse acknowledgement of his words being heeded.

He feels bolder now, for having asserted something, for all that he is sweating, and he keeps his eyes on the selection in progress. Ten more men are standing at the wall now; none of them grey-haired, not one of them, and this is something. But the latest to be chosen is objecting, refusing to step forward, pointing to his family around him. And in the crowd, Pohl hears there is crying.

It is women. They look like mothers; perhaps their sons or husbands have been selected. One or two push their way through the crowd to grasp at Brodnik's shoulders. They might be pleading. Appealing for their men back; or to be chosen as well – not to be separated from their menfolk.

He did not think before he spoke, he did not think; Pohl berates himself. But neither do the women know the kind of work they would have to do if they were chosen.

'It is not women's work,' he calls out. 'It is road work – far too hard work.'

But he sees that his raised voice only confuses. The women

duck and turn at the noise he makes; they do not understand him. He can see from their faces that his shouting makes them fearful. *What is the German saying?* So he calls to Brodnik: 'You tell them. You translate, man!'

Pohl wants it made clear to them.

'They are not strong enough; you make sure they know this. It is not cooks or laundry maids we are recruiting, it is not right to choose them: they will be breaking stones and hauling.'

But the fear and the pleading continue, and so Pohl falters. He has never seen labour teams selected before: *Is it always like this?*

He has long felt uneasy about the work they do; more and more so, as his weeks here have passed and the demands on the labourers have multiplied. The work details break their backs now for so many hours to keep the road to some kind of schedule; they live in barrack bunks for months, eating meagre barracks rations. And now Pohl thinks: *Are they always taken unwilling from their families?* Who would come and toil willingly on this German road of his?

Pohl calls out, across the crowd: 'It is not work fit for women. You understand me? Only the young and strong can do this.'

But even as he is speaking, even as Brodnik is translating, he sees some of the men selected will hardly be strong enough either; not for long, in any case. They will never last out a quarry winter.

So what will happen then, when they are spent? Will they be sent on to rejoin their families? All these young men, taken from their homes and houses; pressed in here together, only to be separated?

'No,' he says then. 'No more of this.'

Although Pohl hardly knows what he is saying.

'Enough,' he says; he has seen enough now to know how wrong this is.

Pohl turns to Arnold, and to the police guards: they are all stopped and staring, but he cannot help himself.

'I will not take them.' He points, refusing the labourers, refusing the Sturmbannführer. A man can only go so far, no further.

'This is not road work,' Pohl tells him, hoarse. 'It is SS work. Yours only.' He will have no part in it, not any longer.

'We are going.' He turns to his foreman. 'This is over.'

Pohl calls a halt.

He takes himself outside. Striding the passageways they were led down, passing the doorways, the smoking soldiers, and then across the factory yard, and along the high wall.

Pohl walks onward – to avoid Arnold, to avoid thinking, to clear his ears of the crying and the pleading. He does not wish to contemplate it further: what he has just seen, what he just been a party to inside the factory. So Pohl walks until he finds himself in the open, out on the cleared ground where they parked the vehicles. He sees mud under his boots and the factory wall behind him, and there, in the cold air, he stops and takes off his glasses.

Bastards.

He curses Arnold; and then the guards and the smoking soldiers. But Pohl knows what must come next, surely.

Insubordination, refusal: the SS will not take kindly.

He presses the heels of his hands hard against his eyes, and he tries a good while to calm his breathing; when Pohl opens his eyes again, he sees it has grown dark while he was inside the factory.

How long was he in there?

Still shaken, and unsure now of his bearings, he sees only dim shapes of trucks and buildings, and then the dark and wide-open cleared ground beyond them.

On the far side, a pool of what looks like lamplight spills across the soil; Pohl sees the yellow glow of this, but little more: a yellow-white blur, over towards the scrubland.

Unsure what he is seeing, or that his eyes don't deceive him – showing him lights where there are none, only a fast-darkening afternoon – Pohl runs a checking hand across his face first, before replacing his glasses, pushing away from the wall to right himself.

His legs are weak as water, palms clammy and useless, but he straightens his collar and tunic: he will not be seen like this. And then Pohl takes another look about himself.

With his glasses on again, he sees the peasant marks of pick and adze in the mud underfoot, where the earth has been cleared of undergrowth, ready for building. It is a wide area he stands before, wider even than he saw from the Sturmbannführer's office, and Pohl's mind turns to the men who must have toiled here to clear it; it would have taken dozens, up to a hundred. And then, turning to the yellow glow, he sees there are labourers over by the far scrub; the SS are unloading trucks there.

They have left the headlamps on, and they are lining

up the workers in the yellow-white beams they cast. Pohl watches them striding between the rows of men. Are they giving orders? The SS look like they're readying them for working, though it must be getting on for evening.

Pohl feels it, like a weight in his chest now: the SS must have their new barracks, new buildings; the territories they have taken must have all the new roads, new houses their vainglory orders. Their plans leave no room for sleep, for adequate meals, for even halfway adequate conditions to work under. Damn the cost to the people.

They do not think on a human scale. They do not think they deal with humans.

These last thoughts are for Dorle; they come at Pohl sharp and fast: what he has just seen in the factory, and what he is seeing even now before him. The lines of labourers in the headlamp glow, and the SS men calling out the orders, pressing them to work, even at nightfall. He thinks, too, of the Jews pressed into the factory. Ready to be used. Deemed useful or removed. His disgust at this wells up again, only to hear that the SS officer has come out to join him.

'Pohl. There you are,' he says, flat-voiced, behind him, from the other side of the yard. And then, when Pohl doesn't turn: 'I've been looking for you.'

The man does not sound angry; his tone is too weary for that. Pohl isn't sure what is coming now – a dressing-down before something worse; some kind of punishment, certainly. But Arnold says nothing further, he just comes to a stop, and he stands and waits there. So although Pohl does not want to, he has to turn then, away from the labourers in the head-lamp glow, and look at the man for a moment.

Arnold blinks a little; he squints at Pohl a little. He is disliked: Pohl thinks Arnold sees that much in any case. And then the officer lifts his shoulders and drops them: a small and sympathetic gesture, where Pohl had not expected one.

But he cannot respond. Pohl can find no words, he is still too disgusted.

'Where the light shines strongest, there is always shadow.'

The Sturmbannführer says this quietly; it is offered like a question. 'Don't you think so?'

'I don't think anything at the moment.'

Pohl doesn't want a conversation. Not with Arnold. And certainly not in riddles about light and dark. What is the man thinking – what on earth does he mean by that? Pohl makes to turn away again, but then Arnold tells him: 'Sorry, I am sorry. I see that doesn't help you.'

He lifts his hands to stay Pohl – not to order, Pohl doesn't think so – just as if to ask him to stay a while. Arnold seems to want to explain himself.

'It is something I tell myself, you see.' He nods, a little self-conscious. 'I say to myself: where there is light, there will be shadow as well. There will always be darkness, and we must accept this.'

But then he sees Pohl frowning.

'Still. I know how it is,' he adds, a little hurriedly, before conceding: 'Sometimes it helps me, and sometimes it doesn't.'

The officer shrugs – hesitant; diffident, even – and Pohl sees that sympathy again. So unexpected from this small man; from anyone in this uniform.

'Listen.' Arnold pauses. Then he rephrases; he tries another time: 'I can see what you think, Pohl. Truly.'

Pohl looks at him, doubtful.

'Even now, I can,' the man insists, surprisingly gently. 'I think much the same myself, you see,' he continues. 'I have much the same thoughts.' Arnold nods.

Then he leans forward, lowering his voice further, as if to confide in Pohl.

'I get my orders,' he says. 'I read them over, and I find myself thinking: *Is this necessary?*' Arnold winces, just a little, before he continues. '*Must we do this?* I have to ask myself, almost daily: *Must it be like this?*'

He points behind himself, to the factory building, to the crowd on the factory floor they have both just come from.

'Must it really be like this?' Arnold repeats himself, this time with emphasis.

The officer looks sincere as he does so; he looks troubled, even. But Pohl can do little more than frown at this revelation, unsure he has heard right, or if he can trust the man.

'I do not like this,' Arnold tells him, insistent. 'I do not like it any more than you do.'

Pohl finds himself shaking his head.

Those people have been herded together on this man's orders; they have been taken from their homes and their livelihoods, to be divided from their families; to be sent who knows where.

'It is cruel, yes?' Arnold interjects. 'Is that what you are thinking?'

'Worse than that,' Pohl tells him.

He is angry now, emphatic. Pohl does not want his

thoughts second guessed; he only wants the man to know how angry he is about this. Pohl wants something done about it.

'How much longer, Arnold? How long are you proposing to keep them pressed in there like animals? The way you treat them. What you SS do here is intolerable.'

Pohl berates him, sore and hoarse. But still Arnold only stands and nods.

'I think that too,' he says. 'I think that also. Just like you.'

And then: 'I feel that it is cruel. Surely any feeling person would?'

He looks into Pohl's face as he speaks, and Pohl thinks he does see pain there. So is the man pained at what he does here?

Arnold is waiting, he wants a response, but Pohl is still so uncertain of what the officer is saying, of where this conversation is leading. He was expecting a punishment for refusing the labourers, not a conversation about the rights and wrongs of misusing the Jews here; and now Pohl doesn't know how to reply, or what the officer is waiting for. The SS man is standing there, shoulder to shoulder with him at the factory wall: a stiff and a dry man – and now a feeling person? Pohl can't be certain of his meaning, but he can feel the officer wants something from him. Is it understanding?

He cannot give Arnold that.

Pohl baulks at the thought.

He shakes his head. He will say nothing; he will do nothing to give any comfort to this man.

So they stand there, wordless, at cross purposes; the factory on one side, the wide and churned ground on the other; and nothing to break the silence between them, save the distant orders still being called out to the labourers in the dark there.

Pohl turns to look at them in their dim circle; the faint glow of the headlamps that falls over their weariness. Where is the bright force Arnold conjures to console himself? Pohl sees nothing of the kind here. Nothing worth the shadows they are casting.

What on earth sort of light does this man imagine is shining?

Arnold shifts a little beside him. He makes a gesture; a strange one, palms open. Hesitant, or perhaps even rueful.

'I don't claim to understand it, Pohl. I only try to endure. I don't know the answer. Perhaps we must all find our own way.'

And then he is dismissing him; he is turning away, ending the conversation. There will be no punishment, it seems; Arnold simply tells him: 'You go now, Pohl. Go on back to your roadworks. You are right about this much: we should not prolong this any further.'

But just as he is turning, he adds: 'There will be a time, you know, when all this is over. This war, I mean. And all these cruelties.'

The Sturmbannführer gestures around himself.

'It is what helps me most, this thought: that there will be a time after. When all of the fighting – when all of this – is done with.'

Arnold holds Pohl's eye, in sympathy, in sincerity, and then he tells him, in parting: 'Perhaps that might help you. To know that all this is passing. For them too.'

He points to the factory, to all the people pressed in there and waiting.

'For them too,' he affirms.

And then Arnold asserts, as though offering Pohl his word, 'This will soon be over.'

Pohl stays well ahead of Arnold on the walk back to the police station. He keeps his back towards him, his face turned away from the SS man, even as they rejoin Brodnik and the rest, and the small company takes leave of one another.

Brodnik is assigned a driver to take him back to the encampment, but Pohl waves away the idea when he is offered the same to deliver him to the boarding house.

He lets the man drive his car, telling him to leave the keys inside when he parks it outside his quarters, and then he walks on alone into the town streets, preferring the cold and the movement, the outside air.

At the boarding house, all the rooms are dark and quiet. Pohl calls for the housemaid and is relieved to be met with silence.

He finds a lamp in one of the low rooms on the ground floor, fumbling for matches in his tunic pockets, and he takes it with him up the narrow staircase. In his room, with the door shut and locked behind him, he places it on the small table, throwing its small light on his pens and writing paper. And then, even before he takes off his coat, Pohl sits himself down to write to Dorle.

He covers pages. All that he has seen and experienced these past days.

You see why I can no longer stand it here? Finally, finally, I have stood some ground now.

It is only because he did this that he can write with such honesty.

Pohl writes the Sturmbannführer's words too, the ones he spoke afterwards, outside on the cleared ground, and he looks at it a good while on the paper: odd, unforeseen, faithfully recorded. Pohl feels again the strangeness of that conversation.

I will put in for a transfer, he tells Dorle. And then: *Arnold can hardly be surprised now, when he gets word.*

Pohl does not know if the Sturmbannführer's office has any say over whether he can leave the territory, or if the man will object; it occurs to Pohl that Arnold may understand his reasons, perhaps.

But he doesn't let himself think too long about this: Pohl wants to think about Arnold as little as possible; what the man might say to his superiors, if he will discuss today's selection with them. *The engineer refused them all, meine Herren; this engineer can no longer be considered reliable.* Pohl cannot mull over such a prospect: it is too frightening.

He sits for an hour, two hours, thinking and working on without interruption, and he keeps going until he is finished, until it is all there on paper, and his fingers are stiff, wrists aching with all the writing.

Inside, there is calm, though. There is a quiet, a strange kind of peace of mind, as though something fundamental has been put in order, finally, for all that he is fearful.

The ink dries on the pages, and he folds them; he addresses an envelope and seals them inside it. And then, spent after the long day and all its revelations, after all he's revealed to Dorle – so much that she will pass on to others too, Pohl is sure of it – he sits a long while, head bent, hands folded in his lap, holding that quiet inside him.

—

In Osip's yard, the wind blows damp at Yasia's skirts. In the workshop, it smells sweet of her mother's apples. Up under the rafters, Yasia finds all is still and dim and silent.

She stands there, on the top rung of the ladder.

'Me,' she whispers into the shadows. And then: 'Food.'

Unsure if she is heard, or if there is no one there now to hear her, she lays what she has brought on the floorboards before she climbs downstairs.

Only long after she lights the lamps does Yasia hear the two boys moving. After she has fed the horse and watered him, and found Osip's tinderbox, setting a blaze in the small stove to warm the pot from the mayor's housekeeper.

The animal flicks its ears, and Yasia lifts her head at the first low creaking of the floorboards above.

She has spent all day in the mayor's kitchens. In the back of her mind, all through her day's work, the idea of them nagged at her: those two boys hiding. If Osip would find them, and if she would be blamed for them. What was she doing, taking in strangers at such a time?

But although she worried, Yasia could not return to check on the boys or to move them on again. She could not look for Mykola either: the town was too full of soldiers. She and the housekeeper heard them passing outside so often, the woman would not hear of her leaving; even after Yasia had finished with the apples, they sat tight together in the kitchen, listening for the next lot, and then the next lot of Germans, waiting for the streets to be quiet enough for Yasia to slip back to Osip's yard gate. She couldn't tell if the men were patrolling, or if they were searching Jews out of hiding, but most were heading for the north side of the town, just as the truck-loads that woke her this morning. It felt to Yasia as though they must be gathering there, out by the factory and the barrack block, and she did not like so many soldiers near to Mykola. She still does not like it.

The yard is in its usual mess. The cart is on all four wheels again in the workshop, but it leans on them strangely, and Osip is sleeping. Yasia found him in his bed, but still fully dressed, and from the depth of his slumbers, and the half-finished repairs, Yasia thought he'd spent the day drinking with the timber man: another wasted day the soldiers have to answer for.

The dark and quiet, and the marsh wind blowing outside the workshop door, added to her solitude, her lonely wish for Mykola. If only he could turn home with her when she goes again.

So when Yasia hears the boys, she is almost glad of them.

Glancing upwards through the gaps in the planks, she sees the older one slipping overhead to where she left the food for them; and then his young face, pale in the gloom of the loft entry, as he stoops over to pick up the morsels.

The boy sees her too, how she sits and watches him. He stops where he is, still half bent over, and then they both blink a moment.

'He did not come?' Yasia confirms, in a whisper, pointing to Osip's back door.

The boy shakes his head, and then he signals: *only once*; Osip came only one time, and he stayed down there by the cart.

'No one else? All was quiet?' Yasia asks him softly.

And he nods to her: they were safe enough in their small conspiracy.

He has the food she left him in his palms, and he lifts it a little as though in acknowledgement. But it looks like far too little to Yasia, especially now she has eaten. The sight of it embarrasses her – nowhere near enough to feed the both of them.

'Wait there,' she says.

She has eggs and flour to take home; paprika too, from the housekeeper's store, and best of all: two long yellow-white slabs of butter. Yasia wants to keep one whole, unspoiled, to present to her mother, but she digs her knife into the other, spreading two hunks of bread for the boys, and then, as an afterthought, another for herself.

Yasia climbs the ladder with the bread in her apron pocket – not all the way, just far enough to reach the slices up to the older one. But once he has retreated, she stays where she is.

The boy sits down with his brother, and Yasia watches them. Leaning against the ladder's slope, against the lip of the entry, chewing her bread as they chew theirs, she whispers: 'Did you sleep?' And then: 'Did you hear the patrols?'

The older one nods in the gloom, and she dips her head in sympathy.

The lamplight seeps up through the gaps in the floor-boards, and Yasia's eyes adjust to the shadows. She sees how the older one takes large mouthfuls, chewing and swallowing. There is ugliness in his eating, ungainly – unself-conscious too, like a small child; he divides the food and swallows his portion hungrily.

On the floor behind him, on the stalk-strewn planks, the younger one crouches, at play with something. He accepts the bread his brother passes, cut into chunks for him with a clasp knife from his jerkin pocket, but he is drowsy, sleep-tousled. Yasia thinks the older one must have kept him still and silent all the day long, let him sleep as long as possible. But that is all to the good, else Osip might have heard them; he might have sent them packing, and she'd have had to answer for it.

And now the curfew is in force again.

'The soldiers haven't gone yet,' Yasia cautions.

She saw more coming through the town streets when she was returning here from the boarding house; far too many to risk putting the boys out. So she tells them: 'You can both stay up here for tonight.'

They will be company. Even if they will be a worry for her; for their family as well.

'Won't your family be looking for you?' Yasia whispers, as the thought occurs to her.

The older one gives her a half-shrug, half-shake-of-the-head, as he turns to attend to his brother, holding out more bread to him. She was only asking, only showing concern, but he offers nothing in return, his face still turned away from her.

'Until the morning, then,' she tells him, short. Yasia is used by now to the townspeople's surliness, even if it irks her. She won't pry further. She shifts her attention to the small boy instead: easier to watch him than talk to his brother.

Crouching and shuffling as he takes his mouthfuls, he ignores the older one's hushed instructions to *sit down, sit still* beside him. This little one has been sleeping the day away, which means he will be awake half the night, and he will be difficult to keep quiet; Yasia knows how little ones are. But at least he plays quietly for now, wrapped up in some whispering game of his own invention.

The lamplight falls on the small forms he plays with: wooden blocks with whittled edges, which he digs from his pockets to place on the boards before him. Yasia sees a house-shaped piece among them, with a steep-pitched roof, or perhaps it is a barn. There are shapes that look like people, almost; ones that look like goats too, or maybe farm dogs; and some others that she can't make out.

In between bites, the small one groups them, and then he leans in to his brother; the two of them whisper to each other, soft – Yasia can't hear what about, she is just too far away to understand them. But she sees how alike they are – and pretty too, as boys go – with their dark eyes and their brown curls and their milk-white faces; in all their milk-white and soft brown fineness. The two boys point to the small forms off and on, nodding and smiling, as though sharing the game now between them.

Osip gave her mending this morning; Yasia promised to be done with it before she set off home again, in return for staying here. But when she looks down the ladder, she doesn't want to sit and stitch alone down there.

The older one glances up briefly as she returns with a basin of eggs and the lamp to work by. He has finished eating, and is sitting splay-legged with some of his brother's toys before him, picking each up in turn with his fine fingers, as though checking them over.

Yasia knocks the eggs against the bowl rim, breaking the shells, and then she begins to peel them, her eyes still on the boys and on the forms that occupy them, and she sees there are more now. A few are neat and painted; they look shop-bought, from somewhere in the town, or sent from Kiev perhaps. But Yasia sees it is the others that the older boy checks over. These are wooden as well, but rougher around the edges; they look home-made to her, or makeshift, and the boy adds a notch here and there, shaping the tops with his knife blade. And then, while the small one watches, the older one produces another from his jerkin – he must have made it for him.

Yasia has an egg peeled and ready for each of them, and she holds them out for the small one to come and take from her, clicking to him rather than calling, until he lifts his head from his brother's work.

The small one edges towards her shyly, reaching for the food. One hand still full of his new toy, he has to give it to Yasia to make room, and she takes it from him gently, pressing an egg into each of his palms in exchange. Such fine little digits; she likes to see them gripped like that, to see all the neatness of his small child's movements. An egg makes a good warm fistful, she thinks, watching his fingers closing around the soft ovals as he returns to his brother's side.

The small boy slips onto his brother's knee to eat and, watching him there, Yasia feels the emptiness of her own lap. Nothing but her own hands to rest there – and even they have nothing to hold in them.

Come the morning, she tells herself: come the morning, she will be with Mykola, she will put her arms about him, even if just for a short while. But for now, she watches as the boys eat and play at the same time.

They sit before her – not too near, not too far away – with

their toys ranged around them. And in the lamplight, Yasia can see the rougher forms all have drawings or carvings on the sides of them: some are taller, some more rounded, but on all are scratchings and etchings. The one the small boy gave her for safekeeping is patterned as well: opening her palm, she sees the blade-marks scored across its surfaces. Turning it to catch the light, she sees these are outlines of leaf and twig and trunk: it is a tree the older one has carved – perhaps all of them are. Yasia looks up to check and, sure enough, the older one has made marks on every one: he has made a forest of sorts for his brother to play with. Or perhaps it is an orchard for his little wooden people.

It seems a strange toy for a town child, and Yasia regards the older one, at watch over his brother's play. But his face is hard to read. He is milk-white and soft brown, but so hard to get the measure of.

The small one has made a tight group of the trees now; there are enough to add up to a good grove – far more than could fit in both their pockets – so Yasia thinks the older one must have spent some of the long day's hiding in whittling more for him.

This thought has her wary.

'Where did you get the wood from?' she asks, lifting her chin, clicking her fingers at the older one and pointing; first at the forms and then downwards, to Osip's workshop and the wood stacks below them.

'You went down there?'

The boy shrugs at her question, hardly glancing in her direction. It might be an apology, but Yasia isn't certain; it might just be surly.

'I said to be careful,' she tells him, curt.

He shouldn't be here at all, so he shouldn't go down the ladder to search through Osip's offcuts.

'I let you stay here,' Yasia reminds him. 'So you should listen to me.'

She points across the yard to Osip's door again.

'He is my father's cousin.' Yasia asserts kinship, authority of some kind. 'What if he'd seen you?'

But still the boy says nothing in response, glancing in his brother's direction instead, putting an arm in front of him – a pointed gesture – as though to shield the younger one from their dispute.

And then Yasia sees how the small one crouches there, contented, taking bites, then lifting and placing the toys before him; keeping up that under-his-breath whispering. An argument would only upset him; it might lead to crying. It might end up waking Osip, just across the yard; the older boy does well to remind her. Yasia tells herself, grudgingly, that he is careful, after all. *No one heard; no one saw him.*

They both fall silent.

She sets to Osip's shirts then, cleaning her fingers of egg-shells, putting the basin to one side; pulling the lamp closer, taking to his buttons and cuffs with needle and thread, while the brothers retreat to the straw on the far side of the roof space. Bent over her mending, Yasia can hear their whispering, but not what they say to one another. It might be a game, or it might just be a story they tell each other about their trees and people. In any case, Yasia thinks the young one will be wakeful for a while still – both the boys will – but they keep their voices low enough, so she doesn't hush them.

She sits up there with them for most of the evening, cross-legged by the lamp with her repairs, her mind wandering as the stove-warmth fills the attic space – to Myko, and tomorrow morning: where best to go and find him. *When the boys are gone.* As soon as she has seen them on their way, she can go to the barrack block; better to seek him out first, before the day is lost to working. She has to see Myko before she turns for home again.

Yasia finds herself dozing, her back against a straw bale, legs pulled under her skirts. She wakes and works, wakes and works, and then nods off again.

It is the small one who wakes her properly. Crying out: she hears him.

Yasia sits up sharply, eyes open, finding herself half in darkness; Osip's shirts still on her lap, needle and buttons lost, scattered across the planks. The lamp is no longer at her side, it is over by the boys – under the rafters, where the small one cries again.

A child's noise, calling out for comfort, for his mother, and Yasia stumbles to her feet as she hears it.

The older boy is quick to stop him shouting. Yasia sees how he presses a hand across his mouth, and he pulls him close too, to try to soothe him. One rough arm about his shoulders, he rocks and he hushes, rocks and hushes. And then he starts up his whispering.

Yasia is closer now, so she can hear him. But she is still confused by the dark and being woken, and the words he speaks sound odd to her; the small one's whimpered replies too. Yasia nears them, and she tries to make out what they are saying – what caused him to shout out? – but it is a strange tongue they speak with one another: murmured and furtive, like a secret they keep between them.

No townsfolk speak like that, none that she knows; Yasia feels she has taken in strangers.

And then this idea sets off a ticking fear inside her.

Are they Jew children?

The boys keep up their murmuring.

Outside it is so quiet now, Yasia doesn't even hear the wind any longer. She strains her ears for sounds of Osip waking, or of patrols – for sounds of anything at all – while the fear ticks on and on inside her, tightening her throat, sending her thoughts falling, one over the next.

If there is no one out there to hear her, no one to see her, she could put the boys out into the lane; send them off down the alleyways and be rid of them. But then the older one glances up at her.

Yasia feels a sudden flare across her cheekbones. He saw her looking; perhaps he saw what she was thinking. She glares at the boy, half to cover her shame, half to make sure he stays silent; and she puts a finger to her lips in warning, still listening for sounds, for signs that they have been heard.

But she cannot put the two of them out, Yasia knows this. And not only because one of them is small and that would be shameful. The whole town is shut down around them, waiting for the soldiers to go again; the neighbours will wake at any noise in the yard, they are bound to look outside, and she cannot have anyone hearing, anyone seeing them leaving. What can she do but let the boys stay on until morning?

Yasia sees that the older one has already drawn the same conclusion. It is there in his eyes: a surprising defiance.

But the small one has calmed a little beside him. He sits blinking at Yasia from the shelter of his brother's arms, and then at the rafters all around them in the lamplight, settling back into his surroundings; and so the older one turns away from her.

He lies his brother down again, keeping his back to Yasia, as though still defying her to put them out of here. She sees it in the set of his boy's shoulders – stiff and insolent in his stubbornness. But he is gentle with his brother, for all his awkwardness, smoothing the child's curls off his forehead, murmuring softly as he tucks the straw like a nest around him. And while Yasia watches him blanketing and covering, inexpert but careful, tender as any mother would, it occurs to her: their Jew mother must have been taken. She must be in the factory, and the older boy knows this.

The thought doesn't help her. Nor does the feeling that this older one sees right through her.

Yasia keeps watch on him, while he lies the small one on his side, pushing the lamp a little closer, so his brother can see his toys again. Piece by piece, the older one gathers all of them together just beside him; and he keeps on his murmuring story all the while too, touching the trees gently with his fingertips as he speaks, ordering them on the planks, opening out the grove, neatening some of the others into two short rows.

The smaller one is still wakeful, but he is settling now in the straw, soothed by his brother's whispers; and Yasia hopes his eyes will soon be closing. She hopes the older one will stop that whispering too, hush that strange tongue of theirs; she would hush it if she could.

Only when the young one's breathing calms enough for sleeping does the older boy quieten. He lets his story tail off then.

The lull that follows eases Yasia's fears a little, as does the sight of the small child's sleeping features. But she stays watchful as she picks up the lamp and retreats to the trapdoor.

She will put the boys out tomorrow. The older one saw that in her face, Yasia is sure of it. But for now he pays her no regard. He doesn't even lift his head as she reaches the ladder, ready to climb down. He stays where he is: half attending to his almost-sleeping brother, half carrying on with his ordering of the wooden shapes before him. His mouth no longer forming words, but his eyes intent as he crouches over them; his face bright with thought, it seems to Yasia. As though he is still telling his story, only to himself this time.

The orchard rows finished, she sees how he pushes the small farmhouse to the end of them, so a neat avenue of fruit trees leads to the carved wooden doorway. Does he imagine a warm hearth behind it, a warm welcome for himself and his brother under those roof tiles?

Where does the Jew child think he will find that?

Yasia douses the lamp, a signal to him to lie down. Be still and silent.

5

Mykola knows well the weight of a revolver. The ones he sees slung from the belts of the SS patrols look around the same weight as the Russian handgun that hung at his own waist. It is only weeks since he felt that; half a lifetime, but only weeks at the same time. He last held the heft of it in his palm when he flung it into the wide Sluch waters, and when he sees the German guns now, he remembers: that heft first, and then the sick mix of fear and relief at being rid of it, crouching deep in the reeds at dusk, waiting for nightfall.

Such a risk he took, deserting. Cutting and running into open country, instead of returning to his unit. It could have earned him a bullet in the back of the neck from either side, if the wrong side had caught him at the wrong time. The Red Army, those black and red Nazis: neither had any care for the wrong and the right of things – or not as he'd been taught them – and Mykola dreaded each as much as he loathed them, all the time he was running. But what other chance did he have of getting home?

The handgun landed deep in the reed and silt at the river's edge, and it gave him a strange lurching feeling to hear it; to be without its weight after so long.

He knew by then what battle was, what battle does; Mykola knew slaughter. He'd seen it in farmsteads and orchards, been in the thick of it on village streets: wherever the fighting ripped through. And he'd seen how it took a grip of men, even those who feared it.

Mykola had stuck with the nervous, the reluctant like himself among the newly recruited, until he'd learned that another man's fear was nothing to trust in. Give the fearful a knife or a rifle, they will use it; in the midst of the fray, give them a flame, they will lay waste.

Soldiers tore at each other; no one wants to die at the hands of another. And Mykola had felt it enough times: his own dark and bastard will to do his worst – and first – before any other man could take him.

But he'd been a soldier then.

And without his uniform, it wasn't soldiers fighting soldiers that frightened him.

Battle was fear and fury, but it was not confined to armies. It tore through fields and barns and houses, and slaughter didn't only take the fighting men. It took all in its wake: the village women, the old and the lame, and the children; all those with no flame or rifle, no reason for soldiers to heed them.

And now he was one of them.

Without his uniform – without his gun most of all – he'd left himself wide open.

Mykola saw others in the days that followed: other deserters, who'd discarded their rifles when they'd thrown off their belts and tunics. Some had left their boots, even, if they were Red Army issue: they'd wanted no trace of that army about themselves, now it was on the losing side.

Mykola had long ripped the badges from his shoulders: they'd been the first to go, landing with his cap in the road-side ditches as he'd started on his way home. He'd stripped away the other remnants over the journey, bartering and begging old clothes to cover him. He'd needed cover then, and food to fill him, so Mykola had taken to stealing; where was the right any longer, where was the wrong in staying alive?

The pistol was the last thing he discarded. For weeks he'd kept his hand on it inside his jerkin while he was sleeping and while he was walking. It had fetched him bread when he needed it, let him rest all those nights he was on his own and out in the open. And all without him firing it. Just the weight of it in his palm had been enough, or the sight of him holding it. The people who saw it held at his side, they knew enough of guns and soldiers, and they gave him food, gave him a bed for the night without argument.

But when the country got familiar, and the people spoke like he did, he threw the thing away. Myko told himself it was best that way. He'd taken it far enough: best it was done with.

He stayed crouched in the reed bed after he'd flung it, even as the dark came; his stomach lurching, palms empty and useless – his hands felt so weak now. But he was on home ground, nearly. Just two days, three more days of walking;

already he was nearing the marshland. He had the wet and welcome smell of it in his nostrils, sunk in the river mud, up to his ankles, and Mykola crouched at the water's edge as the reeling fear subsided, feeling the seep of it through his boot seams, at his heels first, then between his toes, and he was grateful.

He was grateful to be alive still to feel it. And that he'd kept his boots on too, through all of this.

He'd wrapped them in rags to hide them, but Mykola had kept his feet inside them. The boots were Russian, but they were good ones, and they'd eased the long weeks of walking. And once they got him home again he knew he'd need a good pair of boots to farm in.

The ground is soft underfoot where he stands now: where the trees have been torn out, the sod turned over.

Mykola stands shivering on the dog-leg of cleared land, between the back wall of the factory and the scrub where the men were labouring until a few days ago. The sky here is heavy with rain, the earth under him slippery with dead and wet leaf remains, and Myko's boots sink and slide as he stands waiting for more instructions; he waits where he was told, in the cold, by the first of the trucks with the other auxiliaries.

The Germans called them all out, just before dawn, and they are not long out of their bunks and blankets: Stepan and Jaroslav, who were with the Russians, just like him; Taras, who wasn't, and joined the Germans early; he has the bunk above Myko's in the barrack room. But it's not just them out here, it's all the others from the barrack block. Some stand like Myko, hands in pockets, shoulders hunched about their shorn necks, against the raw morning. Others crouch with their backs up against the wheel arches, sheltering from the first spits of rain there, passing the stub-ends of their eked-out German cigarettes between them.

A hip flask has gone hand-to-hand too, along the line and back again; Mykola can still feel the warm burn of his last mouthful, in his throat now and spreading deeper, into his chest, and under everything is the low rumble of the truck exhausts, truck engines.

There are more German trucks out here than Mykola remembers: long parked lines of them behind him, all left idling. So many vehicles, they must have been driven onto the cleared ground in the early hours; Mykola thinks he might even have heard them while he was sleeping. He was still asleep less than an hour ago.

He rubs his face, hard, with the sleeve of his tunic, and then squints across the churned sod at the factory wall before him.

A score of soldiers – more – have gathered by the low doorway where he's been told the Jews are to be brought out. Myko peers at their handguns and their peaked caps, but not for too long: they are SS bastards, and he cannot feel easy around them. After today, Myko hopes they will go again.

All the Jews will be gone in a few hours.

That's what the Germans told them, when they gave out the orders. How much longer until it starts? They have been saying this was coming for days now, and Myko feels caught here, waiting, between the factory wall and the idling vehicles.

He stands at the first row: three grey trucks either side of him, ranked across the mud. All have their tailgates open, their ramps down, ready to receive their cargo, and the narrow gaps between them form a series of passages for the Jews to be passed down. *Rat runs*, Taras told him, as they pulled on their boots and tunics in the barrack room.

All the barrack talk this morning was of the round-up: who saw what, and how many Jews were taken. All the pitiful *zhyds*; the sorry sight they made; especially those that came to line up at the factory, so dutiful, like the SS told them. *Those Germans. Only those bastards could do this.* Round up all the Jews in the district, in their tens and hundreds, and decide they can be rid of them.

'So? Better a bastard than pitiful.'

That was Taras.

'Better to be a bastard, any day.'

Most agreed with him: *Better them than us.* Mykola thinks it is best to get this over with, and so he shifts, waiting on the hip flask's return; the burn is in his belly now, empty of breakfast, and his chest is tight again – all this waiting is making it worse.

Over his shoulder, he watches the policemen passing up and down the nearest of the passageways, talking to the drivers, making last checks. Myko has been watching them make ready, off and on, ever since he took up his position here, and he has been trying to guess at how many vehicles. But the rat runs are too narrow: all he sees is that there are more trucks behind this first row.

Taras has been back there: he says there's a muddy space at the centre, and that the SS have left it clear of vehicles for the Jews to be gathered and counted – they want to be sure they really have got all of them. But more trucks are lined up beyond that; at least another row of them. Myko thinks there must be trucks parked as far as the scrubland, where the labourers stopped clearing. But from where he has been posted this morning, all he sees is the grey of rain on the way, and glimpses of cab roof and tarpaulin as the last few trucks are driven into position back there. If the barrack talkers have it right, there are upwards of four hundred Jews to drive between the vehicles. Jews and their suitcases and children.

'You'll soon see how the Germans do this.'

Taras is on his feet now beside him.

'The Germans have been doing this in all the districts.'

His face is still creased with sleep, but he is wound just as tight as the rest of them, Mykola can see that.

The stubs are all smoked, so Taras climbs onto the ramp beside the policeman, to gain a better vantage. He stands with his feet at Mykola's elbow, craning his neck, looking behind himself, first at the rain clouds and the rows and rows of vehicles, then turning to look over the factory wall before them.

'Can you see them yet?' Myko asks.

Taras shrugs, spitting into the mud. Their trucks are parked twenty metres, more, from the factory, so he won't be able to see into the yard; if there are any waiting there. He's tired of waiting too, Myko thinks. Maybe even the Jews will be.

'Drink, boys,' the policeman tells them. 'Drink, then be ready for them.'

He gestures for his bottle to be taken, to be passed onwards. Older than they are, his face gives nothing away, but even he is watching the factory doorway. On the ramp of the next truck stands another, a sergeant this time, but with the same guarded look about him. Swallowing his mouthful, Myko steps over to reach the bottle up to this next man, and he thinks it might be the same one who woke them from their bunks, even before the dawn came.

'Get up now. Up now. The Sturmbannführer wants this done swiftly.' The sergeant had rapped his truncheon on the bed-frames as he passed through the barrack room. 'We will make this swift, for all concerned.'

That's what the Sturmbannführer told them too, when he spoke to all of them: SS and *Wehrmacht*, police and auxiliaries, all were mustered on the cleared ground this morning. Mykola was pressed at the back with the others from his bunk room, the last to fall in, but he could still make out the Sturmbannführer through the massed heads in front of him. Mykola had seen the man before, driven through the town, driven through the district, conducting inspections, but he'd never heard him, so he found himself listening.

He did not shout, the officer spoke, so there had to be hush to hear him. And when that quiet fell, it held them all – Mykola felt it. He could even see it in the soldiers, that great throng of them, all keyed-up and leaning in to hear the man's intention; and it was the same with the policemen. The officer spoke in German, and mainly to his own men, but

Mykola found himself leaning in to heed the man. Despite the chill out there, and his too rude and recent waking, Myko listened although he couldn't understand even half the words spoken.

He got his orders from the translators afterwards.

The SS at the door will bring the Jews out to them, a few at a time – a dozen at a time, they said – and he and the other auxiliaries are to wait at the ramps to receive them. *Take the luggage and keep them moving.* These first vehicles are for their cases and bundles, and police auxiliaries have been posted at each of the trucks in this first row to do the same thing; all of them from Myko's barrack room.

'You will work fast,' the translators told them. 'This is best. You understand?' Myko nodded; all the others also.

Now Myko holds out the bottle to the sergeant on the truck beside his, but the man doesn't take it; he holds up his own one in answer. Have all of them been issued with a flask this morning?

The sergeant speaks, like he's raising a toast: 'The sooner this is started, the sooner it will be over.'

And then Taras kicks at his elbow, and Myko looks to the factory.

'See them?'

The first to come are few and grey-haired; a small and old group, slow and stooped on the wide mud with their bundles. The police and auxiliaries watch from the trucks in silence as these first Jews look about themselves.

Trapped inside for so long, the old people squint in the daylight, weak as it is, winter's grey-pale light. They peer at the muddy ground, and the rain clouds, and the ranks of vehicles; and there is a second or two of quiet and uncertainty. But Mykola thinks even the Jews want this to be swift now, because once they see the ramps are down and ready for them, they lift their cases, shouldering their bundles: they start making for the vehicles.

No sooner are they moving than the SS run at them.

They peel off from the wall, running hard to set the small group moving faster. This dark and sudden sweep of them has Mykola blinking, pulling the bottle from his lips and wincing as he swallows his mouthful.

'*Marsch! Marsch ihr Juden!*'

The drink burns, and the SS are shouting.

'*Schnell hier!*'

'See what I told you?' Taras's voice is above him. 'See how they make the rats run now.'

Myko can barely hear for the noise of the engines, but he can see how the SS have their mouths pulled wide, faces pushed close to the old men to hound them. And how the men put their heads down, clutching their bags and cases, running as best they can across the ruts in the churned earth.

'We're first.'

The policeman swears as the group is pressed towards them. Pocketing his bottle, shoving Taras down the ramp, he says: 'Be ready. Be ready for them.'

The group are close enough now for Myko to see their faces, crumpled and blinking; their old hands clasped to their cases. One stumbles and falls; another is bent forward, leaning on the shoulders of the man beside him. Bare-headed, a bruised man, his frock coat torn, this bent one limps hurriedly, half carried by his helper. The group struggle on across the mud like this, until the SS bring them to a halt at the truck mouth where Myko is standing; and then all the Jews search the truck backs, anxious – *quickly, quickly* – as though all they want is somewhere to climb inside.

'*Mach schon!*' The SS give the order.

'*Lass sie liegen!*' They are told to drop their bags and leave them.

Perhaps it is the German, or the harrying, or perhaps no one told the *zhyds* this beforehand, but these first few clasp their bundles ever closer, and they look open-mouthed, uncomprehending, from the soldiers who order them to the waiting policemen. They are to drop their belongings here?

'Leave them and move on.' The policeman calls down to them in Ukrainian. 'These first trucks are for your bags. Your bags and cases only.'

These were the orders. Still the men are slow to make sense of this, and they look to the auxiliaries: to Mykola on the mud beside them.

'So it is the next trucks that will take us?' one asks, halting. Dark-eyed, dark-bearded, bent under the weight of the bruised man, he speaks like a townsman. He is not as old as the rest, but his gaze is just as anxious behind his glasses.

'No one told us,' this town Jew says.

Under one arm he clutches a briefcase, with the other he gestures to the bruises, the half-closed eyes of the old man he is holding; and then, glancing between the first trucks to the next row, he asks: 'Must we go far still?'

But Mykola can't answer. He was told: no delays, no talking. Taras is throwing bundles, and already the SS are calling.

'*Nimm die Koffer ab!*' They tell Mykola to get a move on. '*Du, Junge. Mach schon!*'

'You go now,' he mutters to the asking Jew, pointing him between the truck sides as he bends to throw more cases; he was told to throw the luggage swiftly, to keep things moving. But still the asking man stares at him.

'Move on!'

Mykola shouts now, to be heard above the engines, and he makes a grab for the asking man's briefcase: he has more bags from this first lot of Jews to deal with, and already the next lot is being sent out.

'Just go, you hear me? Get moving!'

His throat burns with the noise he makes, not just with the drink now, and Myko glances to the new group already emerging from the factory doorway – can the man not see them?

'This is how it's done, see?'

But the man has no chance to respond. He is shoved, hard and abrupt, away from Mykola by the sergeant; the policeman jumps down from the ramp and slams into him with his shoulder, twice, three times, forcing him to move along.

The asking man has to drop his case, reeling, to keep himself upright under this onslaught; to hold his injured friend also, grabbing him by the jacket sleeve.

Better him than me.

Myko sees his appalled face, his shock at this treatment,

and how he and his bruised friend are harried into the passage between the vehicles. Mykola turns away rather than watch this.

He reaches for the last of the bundles, grabbing at cases, keeping his head low to collect himself. But barely has the asking Jew gone before the shouting starts again.

'*Lass sie liegen!*'

'*Lass sie liegen!*'

Myko sees a mass of shawls and skirts arriving: the second group is run at the truck ramp beside him. More calling, more guards, more German; this time all of the Jews are women, and there are too many bags, too many reaching arms and fingers.

'Drop your things and leave them!'

'Leave them!' Myko finds himself shouting along with the other auxiliaries.

'Get yourselves in order!' The policemen on both trucks call from above. 'Move on!'

'Keep moving!'

After each shout, Myko swallows down the burning feeling, but he can't swallow it all, and the women surround him now. He sees how they lift their palms, taken aback as he throws their cases, but he looks into none of their faces; he wants none of them stopping, and none staring at him like the asking Jew. And although they murmur and mill in their confusion, the women give over their bags as ordered: they've seen the first lot do this and move on.

'Here now? We go through here?' They point, anxious, between the truck sides.

No one told them either, but they don't want to anger,

they only want to find the right trucks to climb inside, so when the soldiers shout them on, impatient, Mykola sees this new group obey them, disappearing quickly between the vehicles.

'This is how it's done, see?'

The sergeant echoes his words at him, dry, seeing his surprise as the women move on and the SS fall away again. Crouching on the ramp to catch his breath, the man passes down his bottle for Myko to drink from.

'Here, boy.'

But although Myko drinks, although he swallows, it still doesn't help him: his throat only stings with the burning drink, and there is so much noise around him. The shouting from the next trucks, the other Jews being hounded, the thuds of the bundles thrown into the truck mouths – and under it all is the roar of the engines.

'Best you drink again,' the sergeant tells him, pointing at the bottle. 'Sturmbannführer's issue. Sturmbannführer's orders.'

Has he done this before? Have the others as well?

Mykola turns to look at the other policemen in this first row, and he sees all his barrack mates are flinging bundles. There are Jews at all the trucks in the line now, apart from his one – and a further group is being run across the mud too. Is there no end to this?

The SS are bringing more; they are bringing them faster, and it is women again, only this time with children. Mykola hears them crying, thin and high, even above the engine noise, while the sergeant leans down to ask him:

'You think this lot will be swift too? Like the Sturm-bannführer wanted.' The man gives a thin smile. 'Did you think this would be orderly?'

Myko doesn't answer.

He doesn't know what he thought it would be.

He takes another mouthful, even if he can't swallow down the stinging or swallow away the roaring. And then he is being ordered.

'You there!'

The policeman on his own truck is shouting; legs broad on the ramp, he points Myko and Taras to the gap between the vehicles.

'You deal with that now!'

Some of the women they just sent running are returning: Myko sees them pouring back out onto the mud between the truck ramps – just as the next lot of women are coming at them from the factory.

'Stop them!'

He has to drop the bottle and run forward, because those first women come flying at him and Taras, appealing, holding their arms out to them and pleading. Myko flings up his own arms, roaring. 'Back! Move back there.'

If he is to keep order, he has to keep them apart from the next lot.

'Back now!'

He and Taras try to head them off, and to contain them – but Myko can't shout loud enough for them to understand him. He has to call above the next set of Jews and their children; above the high noise of their crying as well as above the engines. And he can't get the first women back again between the truck sides: they only shake their heads, vehement, holding out their palms, and they will not pass back again into the gap between the ramps.

'Those are not the trucks. Not the right trucks,' they cry out.

They've seen the vehicles behind this first row, and so they know now: those trucks aren't for them either. The engines are turning over, but their ramps are up and bolted, and no one said this is how it would be.

'Why are they closed to us?'

'Back now!'

Taras grabs at the women to turn them; Myko takes hold of shoulders, handfuls of shawl, too, throwing himself forward. He has to shove at them, tugging and shouting; Myko forces the women back between the tailgates.

Between the truck sides it is darker. But there is no respite, because the women only push back at them harder, blocking the passageway. They turn and cry and gesture; Mykola sees the women turn to each other with questions. *Where are the trucks for us to climb inside?*

'*Lauf!*'

'Get moving!'

'*Lauf, Saujuden!*'

More SS are there now. More have come from the factory. Running at Myko's back, they shove into him and Taras, pushing them, bodily – *Vorwärts! Vorwärts!* – the force of their numbers crowding them further down the narrow space.

Thrust up against the wheel arch in the crush, Myko is pressed in amongst the women he is herding, into their elbows and shoulder blades and frightened faces; too alarmed, too hard up against them. His arms are pinned, legs straining, then he is spilled out onto the mud on the far side – sent sprawling between the truck rows.

He rights himself quickly. Myko feels that grip again, sharp and tight in his fists now: an instinct to lash out as he gets himself to his feet.

But even as he rises, he sees the women are already beyond him. The SS are chasing them along the next line of vehicles, with Taras hard behind, herding them further along the rat run.

'*Schnell hier!*'

Over his shoulder, Myko hears another group coming behind him: it is the same calling, the same raw confusion. *Where are the SS taking us?* Myko has the rough taste of it in his throat now, the chafing feel of it in all his joints; it has him breaking into a run, away from them along the tailgates.

The trucks in this next row are all packed tighter, and he doesn't want to be caught up here by the next lot, caught in their confusion; he does not want to be alone like this either, between the truck lines without orders.

Myko ducks between two vehicles rather than risk that: he has to catch up with Taras. But he cannot press himself fast enough between the high wheel arches; he has to drop to the mud under the truck bed, belly down, scrabbling with knees and elbows, to get to the other side.

When he emerges, finally, the ground opens out around him. Mykola finds himself crawling into a wide space: into the centre, where the Jews are to be counted.

There are still trucks here, but fewer of them, and the

vehicles are parked singly, not in rows: they are dotted across the churned land. And the Jews Myko sees are not running any longer: they are huddled by the trucks in clusters. They are huddled, and the police have got their coshes out.

They hold them in plain sight, calling out new orders.

'You were told. One coat, one jacket. One suitcase of belongings only.'

The Jews are instructed to unbutton their coats here.

'One set of clothes. As you were instructed.'

Those found wearing more must hand their jackets over; they must turn out their pockets, too, and untuck their shirt tails.

'How many shirts did you think you could get away with?'

Such a strange sight, all these crowds undressing, cowed and hasty on the mud beside the truck wheels. The strangeness of it shows in their faces.

Why this? Why this as well?

Don't ask, don't ask. Just get it over with.

Myko scrambles to his feet, stumbling forwards, his hands and tunic muddied; still looking for Taras and for the women he was chasing, he sights a group of women and heads towards them.

The police are taking their shawls and skirts, worn layer upon layer, and they are taking blouses; wherever Myko looks, the police take more and more from them. They must strip to the skin, they are told now, without giving a reason, and some women cry: no one told them they would have to do this either. But others hush them, tugging one another out of their coat sleeves, pulling off their shoes and boots and woollen stockings; their bare soles sliding under them, their bare arms reaching, the first of the rain spitting down on their naked torsos.

Myko sees the jut of their shoulder blades, and he thinks the first Jews must already have been stripped of their clothing. The old men who came first; that townsman who asked him. It must be their clothes he sees piled up there, inside the idling vehicles: that heap of sleeves and coat tails that the policemen are sorting through. But he does not see the old and naked Jews.

Where are they?

Myko looks to the last trucks, all empty, and he feels that clench again – tight and angry, confusing. It has him moving faster, still looking for Taras and a way back: he should not have come this far.

Grabbing at handfuls of clothing as he passes, snatching them from the mud, Myko flings them onto the piles as he stumbles, knowing he should have stayed where he was posted, at the first trucks only: he did not want to see this. These policemen with their coshes raised, and the Jews bent under them. All the people here are ugly in their cowering and in their raging; he hates their fear most of all, and he wants only to get away from them.

Fists still full of rags, he casts about himself for Taras – but then Myko sees there are SS watching over all of this.

Great lines of them are forming: many more than have run from the factory.

Soldiers come on foot from between the far trucks, kicking at the loose shoes and discarded blouses, and they make a wide and watching cordon between the undressing Jews and the last line of vehicles.

They come on jeeps too, and in SS cars, overladen with soldiers, radios blaring. Marches and soldiers' songs ring out across the churned ground as they come driving in from the scrubland beyond the last trucks; men swaying on the running boards, tumbling from the jeep-backs, spilling the bottles they drink from.

Myko sees revolvers held skyward. Shots are fired.

He falls back, instinctive, arms about his head, retreating; these soldiers must have been beyond the trucks the whole time, waiting there and drinking.

Myko falls back further, as the jeeps swerve at the Jews first, and then begin to circle them. He hears the stall and stutter of the engines, and the disordered noise of the men doing the driving; men are still firing. Pistol shots sound out above the music, and the veering sends the discord first one way, then another, echoes reverberating back again from the truck sides, distorted; even the music sounds slurred to Mykola. Men in the cordon are laughing, and he backs away faster from the noise of them and the gunfire; Myko wants no guns pointed near him.

The Jews want no guns near them either: Myko sees them flinching, stripped to the waist and filthy, their faces fearful, turning with the vehicles as they turn their circles. And even if no one told them, the Jews know that this is all wrong, all wrong – but all they want is for this to be over. Myko can see it in their wretched glances, in the way they look all the while to the next trucks, the next trucks – that last row behind the cordon of watching soldiers. He knows that this is their last hope: that when they get to those final trucks, naked and cold, they will surely be allowed to climb inside.

A jeep swerves towards him.

The soldiers in the back are pointing, and Myko picks up his pace, but the driver has seen him, and he veers now to overtake him, as if to round him up.

'*Dein Posten!*'

An SS man drops from the back to stop him. Swaying and grey, the soldier lands on the mud with his arms out while the radios keep on with their wailing, and then he grabs at the clothes Myko is holding, like he is asking, demanding: Well, boy?

'*Wo ist dein Posten?*'

Myko isn't where he was posted; he shouldn't be here, and now this soldier stands drunk before him, taking a fistful of his tunic.

'*Komm Jung.*'

The man starts pulling him across the muddied clothing, and Myko twists against his grip, but the soldier is too strong for him. Too drunk to be listening.

'*Komm nun.*'

He tells Myko to get a move on as they pass the huddled Jews and the line of SS bastards; Myko has to break into a run, almost, to keep up with his striding. And he doesn't know if he's being taken out now or back to his posting; if he's being pulled out for not following orders. The radios blare and the man doesn't turn or explain, he just tugs him further and faster, into shadow between the vehicle sides. Hauling him along the narrow gap between the wheel arches, fast enough to have Myko stumbling – and then out from the truck-lines entirely.

There the soldier drops him.

Mykola lands, hard, and out in the light again: he finds himself cheek down and wincing at the feet of the SS man.

'*Kein schlafen.*'

The soldier leans over him. But it doesn't sound like he is ordering.

'*Augen auf und trinken.*' He dangles a bottle in Mykola's eyeline, like he is offering. '*Es ist bald vorbei, Jung.*'

He tells him it will soon be over; this is all Myko understands. But he is not being ordered. So he just lies where he was dropped, because he thinks this is safest.

Face down, Myko smells the wet soil, newly dug over; the damp of rain on the way, not just exhaust fumes. He can still hear the truck engines and the radios blaring, but both are somehow distant. Around him it is brighter, it is quieter, and Myko thinks if he turns his face away now, then maybe the soldier will leave him. The Germans, the bastards, they can press the Jews between the truck sides without him.

But when Myko turns his head, he sees only uniforms. Such a crowd of them.

Myko sees police and soldiers, and a long trench in front of them. A long pit, shoulder-deep, freshly dug into the soil here.

Four policemen stand with handguns inside the pit; a row of SS on the lip with their revolvers drawn. And at the furthest end? At the furthest end, Mykola sees a tangle of limbs, naked against the mud walls; a heap of thighs and wrists and torsos, of pale skin streaked with mud smears. *All the Jews will be gone soon.*

He lashes out, thrashing about himself.

But the drunk man still stands over him, his dark legs

unmoving, telling him to drink more. *'Trink doch.'* Telling
him it will soon be over.

'Ist doch bald vorbei.'

Myko cannot hear the remaining Jews, but he knows they
are there: penned in by the trucks, that great wall of them,
still roaring; they don't see what awaits them. Not yet, not
yet. *It will be done swiftly.*

'Augen auf und trinken.' The soldier has hold of him, leaning over him, grey and worn and drunken. *'Trink, Jung.'*

Myko pushes the bottle away, but he cannot push it far
enough. And for all that he kicks, for all that his throat is
raw and burning, he cannot fight against him; he can't even
turn his face away. The SS man holds him, and so do the
earth walls, the earth floor, all the men he sees in the pit
before him.

Myko watches, he cannot stop himself, as another soldier
takes up his position, another policeman swings himself
onto the trench floor. The row of men down there is growing
longer, and they pass a bottle too, hand to hand; Myko sees
policemen he knows, townsmen he recognises.

And then, near the end of the row, Myko sees Taras.

His friend has his arm out, reaching, and a handgun is
pressed to his palm by the policeman beside him.

Myko stops his flailing.

He feels the SS man leaning over him, searching his face,
but Myko does not kick against him.

'Ja, du wirst bleiben.'

The man issues no order, he only watches and waits as
Mykola falls still; as though he knows how this works, he's
seen all this before.

'*Erst trinken. Dann auf die Füsse.*'

He says Myko is to drink first, then get to his feet again, and that it will soon be over.

'*Bald vorbei, Jung.*'

Mykola hears the man's voice, and the trucks still roaring; he feels the bottle being pressed against his cheekbone. This time, he takes it.

And then, behind him, Myko hears the Jews driven into the open.

6

Afterwards, there is only quiet.

A grey silence, that hangs over the town roofs, shrouding the lanes and the alleyways.

Osip hears it from where he huddles in his stove corner, how it clings to the house walls and the windows. All around him crouch his neighbours, bent and anxious, come to hide themselves beneath his shutters. They came here seeking refuge, and now they listen as well, breath held. Even the girl is still beside him, although it took such a long while to calm her.

Osip had to pull her in from the yard; he thinks Yasia must have been out there when it started. She was ducked at the yard pump when he first saw her – when the first of his neighbours came pounding at his yard gate – and she had her arms up to shield herself from hearing, but it was as though she meant to shield herself from everyone. Yasia threw their hands off, and she would listen to no one, even once she was inside, shut away from the gunfire, from all those echoes scattering through the town streets, appalling. The girl would let no one hold her. Even Osip could not put an arm about her.

Now she lies curled over – motionless, almost. For hours she has been like this. But Osip stays where he is beside her, and he thinks that she must hear the silence, even so; that it is over. She must know that the soldiers are done here, surely.

It comes over them like a numbness. Like a deadening, come to cover them. Osip shuts his eyes and feels the weight of it, stone cold and quiet, falling across the town, the wide and flat lands around it. Sinking into the cart ruts, the ditches at the waysides, into all the cuts and the trenches. It presses down on everything around him. The beams and the lintels; settling into the gutters, even, and the runnels between the yard bricks.

No one speaks; no one dares yet, but Osip knows that they all listen for the same thing: the roar of the trucks starting up again and driving. The sound of the soldiers leaving the town behind them.

But the quiet goes on for so long.

Why don't they go now?

Why can't they leave us?

Osip crouches and waits with his neighbours; and he sees it in their eyes, how they listen and wait, just as he does. But still they don't hear it – and how long have they been waiting here like this?

In the stove, the fire has burned down to embers; outside, the day is already darkening. The town is shuttered and bolted, all the townsfolk hiding, but there is only the silence, leaden and cold; nothing to tell them what the Germans will do now.

7

Yasia lifts her head at the sound of movement. A rustle of skirts, uneasy; a shifting and a standing around her.

Stiff and slow from so long curled over, she squints and finds not Osip beside her: just neighbours, furtive in the half-light, and then the door being pulled ajar, and the wind blowing in across the yard.

There are voices outside – Yasia hears whispers. Strange to hear them after so long spent in silence. She thinks the neighbours must have heard them; it must be those voices that have them standing, going to listen at the open door. But although she pulls herself to her feet as well, Yasia is slower than those around her; she is amongst the last to reach the doorway and to peer out into the darkening yard beyond it.

Some of the neighbours are already on the yard bricks, others are darting forwards, cautious, to join them. Still caught up with the rest, Yasia peers towards the workshop, looking for Osip: she doesn't like this crowding, or how the whispers are getting louder, and she would sooner have him near her.

The timber man is out there. His wife too: Yasia can just make her out in the shadows by the yard wall. Is she the one whispering? Her voice is a sharp hiss, but Yasia can't see her face yet. Her husband is at her shoulder, as though he has to hold her – is she angry? – and the neighbours are clustered about them, a nervous half-circle, with Osip at the centre.

Osip.

As soon as she sees him, Yasia presses forward. Except the timber man's wife is still getting louder, and then Osip throws his arms out.

'Quiet now!'

This has Yasia halting, holding back a moment.

'Mind yourself.' Yasia hears Osip's warning. She sees too, how he casts looks around himself as though for listeners at the windows. But the woman won't be hushed.

'I heard them,' she insists, stepping forward, taking Osip by the elbows. 'You think I am the only one?'

Is she talking about this morning?

The last of the neighbours push past Yasia, but she stays where she is on the yard bricks, still only just grasping what is happening. What is the woman saying?

'Why haven't the soldiers gone now?' The woman is insistent. 'They're still looking, Osip. Don't you see that?'

Yasia can see how she holds him, forcing him to face her.

'You have some here,' she tells him. 'Don't lie to me. I know you do.'

And then she gestures to Osip's workshop, and Yasia's insides tighten.

She is talking about the two boys: she must be. About the Jew boys under the rafters. Yasia glances up there, knowing she has left it far too long to go and see about them – that it may be far too late now.

'And if the Germans come?' the woman demands. 'What if they come calling?'

'Enough now!'

Osip pulls himself free of her, stepping back, shaking his head at the timber man, and then at all the neighbours who surround him.

But even while Osip protests, Yasia sees – as he does – that already some are retreating. They are turning for his gate, or slipping through his broken yard wall, and already Osip looks less certain. He can see he stands alone here.

'Be careful,' the timber man issues a warning, retreating himself now: 'If we don't say, then someone else will. You can be sure of it.'

He pulls his wife after him, but she won't back down yet, turning to Osip as she is leaving.

'You look in your workshop. You ask that one.'

The woman points at Yasia – straight at her – before she can duck away from the doorframe.

So Osip sees her watching there.

Soon Osip sees everything.

He climbs the ladder and finds them: both boys in the straw bales.

The small one cries out as he pulls away the blankets, but Osip barks at him sharply.

'Hold your mouth now!'

Shocking him into silence.

He stares at the children first, curled together like mice under his rafters, and then at Yasia, come to a standstill at the trapdoor. Osip sits down, hard, on one of the leaking bales, head in his hands and groaning, fingers gripped to his forehead, appalled at what he has uncovered here.

'I didn't know,' Yasia starts.

But Osip does not look at her; he does not even lift his head. He is so quiet, Yasia doesn't know what she can tell him.

The boys needed hiding so she hid them, they needed feeding so she fed them; that was all she was doing. She didn't know about them. She didn't know. Or what the soldiers would do to the others.

But Yasia can't let herself think of soldiers, because then she will think of Mykola. She looks to the two boys instead, but that just makes it worse: seeing them held tight to each other between the straw bales. Their white and stricken smallness. Did they hold tight like that all morning? The two boys must have heard it, just as she did.

As soon as Yasia thinks that, she has to turn her face away.

Below them, the last of the neighbours are scattering: a clattering of boot-soles out into the alleyways. They heard Osip shout; that was enough.

'She will bring the police,' Osip breathes, pointing down into the yard, in the direction the timber man's wife ran, just a few moments ago. 'She will bring the Germans,' he says. 'She will bring the Germans. If someone else hasn't already got there.'

The older boy has already understood as much. He heard

the neighbours turning tail, and now he starts crawling past Yasia, tugging his things together on the floorboards: his jacket and hat, his brother's scattered toys. Stuffing all he can into his pockets, throwing the rest down to the workshop floor below them – boots and blankets tumbling – he pulls his brother from the straw and onto his shoulders.

Osip won't look at Yasia. Head in his hands and wretched, he doesn't look at the two boys either, as the older one clambers down the ladder with the young one clasped tight around him. Osip only holds his face gripped in his fingers, so Yasia gropes her way behind the boys; half falling down the last rungs in her confusion, she follows them almost blindly.

The older one is grabbing at the blankets when she gets to the workshop floor, tying them into a bundle, his face aflame, eyes averted, as though he expects her to shout now and send him running. Yasia watches him, the way he turns from her: not defiant, not any longer, only frightened. He didn't know either: that the soldiers would do that.

But Yasia has to fill her thoughts with something else now.

She tugs one of the cloths from her mother's basket, laying two apples in the middle; eggs and a heel of bread to send the boys away with – except how long that will last them? Not even a day, not without hunger. And how long will they need to hide for?

She looks up again to find the older boy at the doorway. He still has his young brother clutched to his shoulders, and he is trying to hold him there, tying a blanket around them both to bind him; so he can run with him, maybe. But the knots are difficult and the younger one shrinks from the wind blowing in damp from the marshes. Where can they hide where they will be warm enough?

'You have to go now.'

Osip cut across Yasia's thoughts. He is standing, stone-faced at the trapdoor.

'You have to leave,' he tells the two boys, as he comes clambering down the ladder's rungs, lumbering across the workshop floor. 'You should never have been here in the first place.'

He still can't bring himself to look at them in more than glances, though Yasia thinks he must see how frightened they are, surely. He can't just send them out onto the town streets; they can't just do nothing for them. But when she makes a move to implore him, he brings her up short.

'We have to go as well, child,' he tells her.

Osip gestures at his yard, now empty of neighbours, and his fingers shake with anger.

'You think we can stay here?'

Yasia still has the food she wrapped, she holds it dumb in both her hands, while Osip tells her, 'You're not safe, child. I'm not safe either. Don't you see that?'

And then she sees he is fearful; it is not just fury making his fingers tremble.

Osip steps towards her. 'If the Germans find *they* were hiding here. What do you think they will do to us? To *us*, child?'

Yasia has no answer to that. She can only shake her head, while Osip takes a step back again, his eyes darting around himself.

He surveys his surroundings: eyes flitting from the horse

in his stall to the boys in his doorway, and then to the half-repaired cart by the workshop wall. Yasia can see how frightened he is, but that he's working something out now. So even if he is angry, she hopes that Osip will help still: he might know how to help the boys. When he goes to lift the harness from the workshop hooks, Yasia takes a step towards him.

'Who can we go to?' she asks, low and careful. She doesn't know the town nearly as well as Osip does, or the townsfolk; who would keep them safe now?

'I will find someone,' he mutters over his shoulder. 'I will have to.'

Then he turns to her. 'But you can't come with me,' Osip warns, stopping her from coming closer.

'No, girl,' he halts her. 'You can't come with me. I said it already: you're not safe for me to be with.'

He keeps his distance – not just from the boys, but from her as well – and then he tells her, 'You can't go home, either. Don't you be thinking that you can go there.'

Yasia stares at him, dismayed: what is he doing? What is he saying? But Osip will not give way.

'How can you go home now?' he asks, turning on her, his eyes sharp, hands gripped hard to the harness. 'What if you bring the Germans after you? Would you do that to your mother, your brothers? Like you've done to me, girl. Over *those* two?'

Osip points at the boys by the doorway.

'They were *heard*,' he says, despairing. 'You were *seen*, child. How could you do it?' he demands, throwing up his arms.

Yasia thinks he will throw the reins at her, and she holds herself in readiness.

But then he falls a little quieter, dropping his arms again, checking around himself. Osip stands, slack-shouldered, in the silence that follows this. At a loss. As if he can't find the words. What more he can say to her?

The boys stand silent also: the younger one pale inside his blanket binding, the older one no longer making to run; his face no longer turned away from them either. His eyes are dark and frightened, but his gaze shifts, alert, between Osip and Yasia.

'You have the horse,' Osip says at last. 'You can have the cart, too.'

He points across the workshop, holding out the harness.

'You go to your uncle's,' Osip mutters. 'Your mother's people. You go to the marshes; you've been there enough times.'

It leaves Yasia helpless. She stands on his workshop floor as he casts about himself.

She knows the tracks to her uncle's village: Yasia has trekked the two days, three days, almost every year of her childhood, overnighting by campfires, under blankets, with her mother and her brothers sleeping around her. But only ever in the late-summer warmth, in the dry weeks after the harvest, before the leaves start turning.

'It's too far,' Yasia starts: it is too late in the year for such a journey.

'So? So?' Osip cuts across her, throwing the harness to land beside her. 'You have to. You have to go where no Germans are. Don't you see that?'

He has no time left for arguing, and he strides away from Yasia's pleading. The older boy ducks from his anger, but Osip shoves at him as he passes, forcing the brothers into the yard before him.

'Get away from here,' he orders, rough now, a low growl. 'You stay away from me – and away from her.'

The older one scrambles away from him along the yard wall and Yasia wills him to be faster, even as she sees his face turning, still keeping watch on her from the dusk outside. She wants the boys to run far away, and for Osip to turn and help her.

But Osip tugs the yard gate open, he slips out into the darkness, without another glance in Yasia's direction; and then all she can see is the cart by the workshop doorway, listing on its axles, and the harness before her on the floor in tangles. All that she can think is that she has to go to the marshes. That it is too far, it is too cold and dark.

But how long till the timber man's wife finds a German, finds a policeman – how long until they get here?

Unwashed, still in yesterday's clothes, Pohl emerges from the boarding house into the lane beside it.

He has been waiting for quiet and nightfall; Pohl needs to be far from here, to get to the encampment where he can think again. When he sees the car is still where the SS driver parked it, under the dripping overhang of the house front opposite, he checks the lane around him, taking a firm grip of his cases, and then he slips across cobbles towards the vehicle.

But a noise – in the lane ahead – has him halting. Startled, he lifts his face; Pohl thinks he hears movement. He stays where he is, stiff and guarded.

All day he has felt watched. He has feared that Arnold or the Gestapo would come calling. Pohl lay in his quarters, reeling, after what he heard this morning.

First came the shock, and then the slow and dread realisation: if they are capable of that – if they are capable of that – then he too might be taken.

Out here, they can do anything they want. There is no law or truth or trust, no sense of reason; there is no one he can turn to either. He's left himself wide open. So Pohl stands now, taut and alone, facing the gloom in the lane beyond him.

But the houses here lean in to one another, and he cannot see anything between those dark walls; all he hears is the dripping from the eaves, water trickling along the guttering.

'Who's there?' Pohl whispers, hoarse, accusing.

His voice is loud in the quiet, but gets no answer.

All day, Pohl did not rise or dress, or eat or wash; he could not even close his eyes. It was cold enough in the room to see his breath, but he lit the stove only long enough to burn his letters, the words he wrote to Dorle, just the night before, which now seemed so hollow to him.

He could have taken twenty, thirty, forty. He could have selected so many – men and women both: they wanted to be chosen. But he refused them. He did nothing. And Pohl could see nothing on the pages but his own pride and blindness; nothing but a rope to hang him with. So he stuffed the papers in amongst the kindling, holding a match to the nearest, watching them catch and curl and blacken before retreating.

Those words will not be read now, by anyone. As soon as he gets to the encampment, he'll burn the rest; the authorities will have no written proof of his dissent. But Pohl knows, too, they will not need that.

And now – again – he hears something moving.

But not ahead of him in the darkness, as he'd first thought; Pohl feels the noise is coming from behind him, from beyond the lane mouth.

Someone is approaching from the town square.

Pohl turns his head at the sound of footfalls: not just one or two – it sounds to him like a group – and his stomach lurches at the thought of those coming for him.

He knew there would be patrols in the town this evening; Pohl had reckoned on policemen enforcing the curfew, and he'd steeled himself for clearing at least one checkpoint. But if this is not policemen. If this is Gestapo, he is lost now.

He opens the car door, throwing his cases across the driver's seat, but Pohl knows he has no way of escaping, so he straightens up again, to brace himself for questions – for arrest, even.

And – just then – Pohl hears the first noise another time.

A muffled shifting; a stifled breath, perhaps.

It is closer to him, this first noise – and it is coming from the dark in the lane beyond the car, where he'd first heard it. Pohl turns towards it, unnerved to feel it so near now; to feel himself surrounded. There is a unit on the square behind him – police or Gestapo – and someone ahead too, in the darkness.

'Who's there?' he repeats, a frightened hiss. And then: 'I can hear you.' He wants no one playing games with him.

Pohl gets no answer, but someone is there and waiting. Maybe it is even more than one person, readying themselves to taunt him. Pohl reaches inside the car, fumbling for the lever, flicking on the headlights.

The lane is bathed in white light.

And it is children: three children he finds there.

Dishevelled and frightened, peasant children by a horse-drawn cart, leaning crooked on its axles.

They are pressed to the house walls, half hidden by the turn in the lane, but Pohl sees a girl – almost grown – at the horse's head, and two boys following. One of school age, nearly as old as the sister, but the other far younger, squinting and frightened, swaddled in blankets, bundled on to his brother's shoulders.

The horse's hooves are wrapped in sacking, the girl's boots also. They have been caught out under curfew, caught in the headlights of an SS car, and the girl stands frozen. The older boy only hesitates a moment – just long enough to seek Pohl out, to see who he is faced with – and then a shout from the town square has him alerted. Already the boy has his head up, eyes wide and darting. The footfalls are closer, the voices louder; it is too late to run now, and the child turns his gaze on Pohl again, fierce in the white light, as though Pohl has snared them.

But Pohl is just as caught, and he shakes his head at the children, motioning for silence, for their compliance. He holds up a warning palm, and they flinch at his gesture, but Pohl reaches into the car, turning off the headlights.

The lane and the children are swallowed again by darkness.

The seconds pass then.

Pohl stands in the black, breath caught in his throat, listening for the unit still approaching.

All is so quiet, so still in the lane before him; the children are silent, and the walls so close and dark around them, he finds himself pleading: *Let it be a patrol; let it be a patrol, not Gestapo.* Because if it is a patrol, they may just pass him. In the dark there, this seems almost possible.

Pohl sees the torch beams.

Khto tam?'

He hears the voice come.

'Vidpovidayte!'

And the voice is Ukrainian.

The tone is blunt, but they are policemen. They are not Germans, Pohl is sure now, and this is something at least.

'Nehayno!'

But still the voice comes curt, demanding an answer, and Pohl feels the children shrinking, anxious, beyond him. If they run now, they will draw the patrol; these men will come after them, and who knows how peasant children will be treated?

When the policemen shout again, Pohl answers: 'Engineer.'

He calls to them, over his shoulder: 'Reich engineer.' And then he turns to them.

The policemen mutter at the sound of German. They silence one another as he steps forward, and they shine their torches into the lane mouth, searching.

'Here!' Pohl tells them: he has to stop the beams lighting on the children. 'Over here,' he calls again, still advancing towards the policemen.

He waves his arms to draw their torches, and finds himself blinded; Pohl lifts his arm higher, half to shield his eyes, half to show his armband, but he keeps on walking.

'Reich engineer, I told you. So you can drop your torches. Drop your torch beams,' he orders, sharp and squinting in their harsh glare. 'I am in charge of the road-works here.'

The policemen hear his tone, and they see his uniform as well now, so they lower the beams, lowering their voices.

'*Mein Herr*. My apologies.'

One of them speaks German; the man takes a step back as Pohl draws closer.

'We did not know,' the policeman tells him. 'We only saw the light here.'

'You saw my headlamps, that is all.'

Pohl doesn't get too near, stopping just close enough that they can see him by the town square street lamps. The glow these cast is misted, but Pohl can make out the men too, now that their beams are down: their hunched shoulders, tired glances, collars pulled up against the damp night falling. It is getting colder again after so much wet, and there will be a frost soon, Pohl can feel it. The men look at him, weary, faces worn by long hours of patrolling.

'Apologies.' The German-speaker repeats himself; and then the man collects himself, remembering his patrolling duties: 'You are coming back to the town, *mein Herr*? Or just leaving?'

'Leaving.' Pohl is short. He wants no conversation. 'Who is in charge here?'

'Me,' the German-speaker tells him.

His voice is flat, as though he feels little enough at this distinction. Pohl thinks: they are country policemen, who carry no revolvers; perhaps they were not part of this morning. Even so.

'I have a car here,' he tells them, gesturing into the dark lane behind him. 'I had the headlights on, as I told you. Nothing more.'

'Yes, *mein Herr.*'

Pohl thinks these policemen may be the only ones left to patrol here. They have been left to keep order, he decides, where there is none. But he smells drink on their breath. And he does not want them asking his name, lest he is already on a Gestapo list.

'Do you need my papers?' he asks, already half turning. 'Or may I go now?' Pohl tries cutting this encounter as short as he is able.

'No, no. You can go, *mein Herr,*' the policeman tells him. 'Good evening.'

Pohl can feel the men making ready to retreat again, relieved to have this over with; they begin to turn away, even as he nods to dismiss them.

'Good evening.'

Almost at the car again, Pohl looks one last time – a half-glance over his shoulder – just to be sure the patrol is walking on now. As soon as he sees they are gone, he finds his hands are trembling.

Pohl stops by the open car door. He has to let himself stand a while: his breathing difficult, his wrists weak, his eyes adjusting again to the darkness.

When he looks up into the lane, he finds the children are still there.

He can just make them out: the girl holding the horse, the older boy behind her, silent and guarded. Pohl sees the way they look at him, the way these peasant children take him in: ashen, unshaven, he is a German. He sent the police away. But they don't trust him.

Why should they? Pohl steadies his breathing, telling himself they have no reason. But he does not like the way they keep watch on him after so much confusion; he finds himself provoked by their staring, especially the older boy.

'Why are you out here?' he whispers, half turning to address him.

No one should be out at such a time; even these children know this, else why would they be hiding?

'Curfew,' Pohl tells them, addressing the girl as well now. 'Curfew, remember?'

He speaks more sharply than he intended, but the children blink at him, so distrustful.

'It is madness to be out here,' he tells them, and it comes out with such harshness – but it was such a risk he took for them, diverting the policemen.

'Should I have let them take you?'

They don't understand the words, but they hear how ugly they are, and they watch his gestures, apprehensive, as he lifts his arms from the car door to the surrounding houses: they should be inside, not wandering the lanes here.

Pohl holds his palms out, angry now, like a question. 'What on earth are you doing?' he demands. 'Where on earth do you think you are going?'

'*Bolota.*'

Marshes. It is the boy who says this.

He ventures that one word, squinting. Just one, but Pohl knows it.

'*Na bolota.*'

To the marshes; the boy risks it another time, pointing north, beyond the town, then pulling his arm back again, sharp, and watching for Pohl's reaction.

But the girl is the one who moves first. She turns to her brothers, alarmed, glancing at Pohl, shaking her head, hissing something at the older boy – imploring – as though to stop him talking. As though Pohl should not be told this.

And then Pohl finds himself uncertain: who is this boy before him? A marsh farmer's son; are these marsh farmer's children? Or is this a partisan brood, sent to bring back weapons and food? He could have been covering for anyone.

The way the girls entreats them is so vehement, it has Pohl blinking in his turn. It is as though she means to send both boys running away from him – but away from her as well, through these dark lanes. And what good would that do? Does she want them in the arms of that police patrol? The small one wrapped in blankets is too young for such dangers, surely. The cart the girl leads is all but empty, it stands listing on its axles, and when Pohl sees this, he thinks they are not outlaws; all he can see is their poverty, their rags and blankets, and then he has no time any more for their squabbling.

'*Na bolota*?' he demands, commanding their attention, taking a step towards them.

The older boy recoils then, instinctive, making to run from him – and then all the confusion spills out of Pohl as anger.

'No!' he barks. 'Don't! You listen to me!'

He wants an end to this, and swiftly. Pohl strides forward, reaching for the boy, taking hold of his bundle. He rips it from his arms, and he flings it inside the cart, pointing the child to climb inside there, hissing at the sister to get them moving.

'Move now! Why don't you get away from here?'

But the boy retreats further; Pohl has to lunge at him to stop him. His fingers close on jacket first, and then on arm and blanket, and the boy kicks against him, limbs flailing, but he is slight and Pohl is angry; he starts hauling him.

The child on on the boy's back cries against his grip, twisting inside his binding, but Pohl only grasps them tighter, dragging them back regardless. They shouldn't run from their sister, they should go with her, and he wrenches them so hard across the cobbles, both children almost fall as they get to the cart side. There Pohl hoists them, rough and forceful, righting them first, then shoving them over the low rail onto the planks. He holds them down too, on the boards, until they stop their flailing.

But when he sees how they lie there, shocked and silenced – the young one's face pressed into his brother's neck, and the older one breathless – Pohl feels how hard he holds them. He sees too, how the older child looks at him, his eyes wide with fury.

Pohl has to let go then, breathless himself.

He glances at the sister, jarred at his own behaviour; then

Pohl retreats to the car, pointing her along the lane, away from him once again.

Still unwilling, she eyes his gesture; all the more mistrustful after the way he dragged the boys, the way he held them down. It is as though she expects him to give chase now, or shout for the policemen. But she makes no appeal this time, she just obeys him.

The wheels creak as they start turning, and the cart tips on the cobbles, but the horse's hooves barely make a sound, wrapped in their layers of sacking, and the girl's boots are even quieter.

The small one turns his face away from Pohl, fearful, as they pass, lying curled against his brother in the cart. But the older boy keeps watch on him, his eyes fierce and dark, as the cart retreats ever faster, and Pohl has to turn away from that stark gaze even before they reach the corner.

8

They flee in the darkness. From the lane and the square and the German.

The jolting is terrible, and the noise they make, the cart wheels jarring; curled tight around Momik, Yankel hears the rattling thrown back at them by the house walls. He still feels the man's grip on his arm; he feels the way the German hauled him. It is a bruising, between shoulder and elbow, and it is a twist inside him, fierce and furious, at being hauled about and ordered.

Yankel rages at that rough handling; at the clatter of the wheel rims against the cobbles, and the way the cart pitches under them: he is sure they must be heard, that they will bring patrols tearing after them. The cart is so thrown about, all through the town streets, Yankel has to brace his legs against the planking. It is even worse as they pass the last of the houses, the girl pulling the horse far too fast down the incline to the orchards, her rag-wrapped boots, the animal's rag-wrapped hooves sliding under them.

The cart lunges across the bridge, and then at last Yankel sees it: the dark town falling behind them. But it can't fall fast enough for him.

He searches for shapes in the black, shadows at the few small windows, narrow and lamp-yellow and receding; looking for watchers, for anyone following. His thoughts still full of the German with the glasses, he watches for headlights, for torches – and Yankel wants only to get to the marshes. The man in the workshop said no Germans go there; the schoolmaster told Yankel only the partisans have held out against the invaders. So Yankel can't rest now, not until he and Momik are on partisan ground: he has to take his brother where no Germans can find them.

They pass under branches, hiding the scant lights from view; the next time Yankel sees the town lights they are already growing fainter. The night thickens around them, tree and scrub growing ever more densely at the track sides as they pass out into open country.

The girl drops her pace as the lights dim behind them, but just enough to stop the cart lurching; still she pulls the horse onward – and still Yankel watches; even after there is nothing to see back there, only dark behind and dark ahead.

For hours it is like this.

Long after they have put the town behind themselves, the night stretches out seemingly endless around them, a cold mist rising from the verges, settling across the cart track they follow.

Momik whimpers, unsettled by the darkness. Shaken and

cold, he cries for his bed, and for their mother to carry him there, and Yankel pulls him close, but roughly, and only to keep him quiet. He cannot bear to listen to all he cries for, but he cannot soothe him either; his thoughts are still so full of fury, and of who might be setting out to find them. Yankel's bones are jarred too, the planks shifting beneath his hips and shoulders. He hears the axles groaning, feels the wheels too loose and leaning, but he cannot bear to go slower: he is certain that they will be followed and found and hounded. That they won't have got far enough before the dawn comes.

The girl throws the reins across the horse's back, and clambers up onto the seat to drive him, hissing him onwards, reins gripped tightly. But Yankel cannot trust her. She never looks at him or Momik, despite Momik's crying: she only sits there, silent, on the cart seat above them.

Yankel fears she will stop; that she will turn them out onto the ground here – run for the marshes without them. Yankel doesn't know now: if she is a farm girl, if she is a marsh girl, or how far she will take them. He sees only that she doesn't want to be found either, because she doesn't let up, not even to rest the horse.

The animal tries refusing, digging in his hooves, stiff-necked, stiff-legged, but the girl will not allow it. Each time Yankel feels him halting, she drives him on further, and when the horse's tread gets more laboured, she slips down to take his head again, tugging all the harder at the bit clamped between his teeth. Even when the rags come loose from her boots, from the horse's hooves, the girl doesn't stop and tie them.

But she has to stop when they reach the wide cut of the roadworks. The animal pulls up short and snorting on the mud before it, jolting even Momik into silence; and then the horse just stands there between the shafts, his old flanks heaving.

Yankel sees the rubble piled high before them. It is a long embankment that slopes sharply upward, and there is no way round it: the rocky bank stretches onwards in either direction, into the distance, where the night sky is already greying.

The girl sees it too, pulling at the reins again. But the horse throws up his head rather than crest the roadworks, and the girl flings her arms out, hurling the reins at him.

She tears the rags away from each of his hooves in turn, and from her own ankles too, flinging the clouts away from herself, and Yankel thinks she means to force the animal. But then she steps forward, without a word, without even a glance at Yankel, and unbuckles the horse from the shafts.

The cart sags without the animal to hold it upright; Yankel has to grab at Momik to stop him sliding, as the oilskins and blankets slip onto the mud below them. The food bundles fall too, landing in the wheel ruts, but the girl still keeps her back turned, all her attention on the horse.

Yankel scrambles to the ground, tugging Momik down after him, because the animal shies again, slipping and lunging, as the girl leads him from the cart-side. Yankel has to step in front of Momik to shield him, and to pull the bundles clear of the horse's hooves.

He crouches down beside his brother, wrapping him in one of the blankets, telling him to be quiet now, to stop his shivering, not to start up again with his whimpering; but Yankel keeps his eyes on the girl, too, the way she cajoles the horse, impatient, walking him up and down between the cart-side and the roadworks. He can't be certain: how long she means to rest the animal from the cart's weight, or how long until dawn comes.

Is this it now? Yankel looks about himself at the greying night – is this where she will leave them?

The long rubble thoroughfare is deserted, but the mud beneath his feet is ploughed with spade marks and tyre prints. Yankel knows they have to be gone before daylight – because with the light will come workers, and it must be Germans who watch over them. Perhaps it is even soldiers.

He takes Momik by the hand first, pulling him along the foot of the rubble sloping before hoisting him onto his back and tying the blanket firmly around them both. Yankel scans the roadworks, but he can see nowhere low enough for the cart to pass; he knows that nowhere this road leads will be safe enough – only the far side; only the fighters' ground. But then he looks back to the girl again, still tugging at the horse's head, and he can't be sure that she will take them there.

The girl is hauling the horse back to the cart, but the animal kicks out rather than back into the shafts, hooves cracking hard against the planks. Momik cries out, pressing his face into Yankel's neck, frightened by the horse and the noise and by the marsh girl's anger; when she flings her arms wide again, Yankel flinches at the sight of her.

He stoops for the bundles. Yankel snatches as much as he can reach, as much as he can manage – a cloth-wrapped loaf, an oilskin, apples tied in a scrap of sacking. And then he turns and runs with this armful before the girl can see and stop him.

Lurching under Momik's weight, the oilskin trailing, he clambers up the rubble, tripping and sliding. Yankel drags himself forward, heaving them upwards, Momik grasping tight to his shoulders, all his small noises, small movements fearful.

'We have to climb over,' Yankel tells him, full of anger as he scrambles. 'We have to go where no Germans are.'

His head is filled with thoughts of daybreak and of soldiers, and with those thoughts come so many others: of the German with the glasses, of the bruising grip that held him. They set off that same twist of fear and rage inside him – fiercer now – and Yankel thinks he will never be hauled again: he will not allow it. Yankel thinks all the thoughts he hasn't been allowing himself: how the soldiers must have hauled his sister, his mother; his father. His father who lined up for the Germans. Yankel reaches behind himself for his brother, pulling at the blankets that bind them: no Germans must ever haul Momik.

He clambers over the ridge, half tumbling, ankles twisting under him; he has to put a hand out to the rocks to keep himself from falling as he starts on the downward slope. But Yankel knows he must keep going.

He has to find the fighters' ground, and then he will go further; he will find a place for him and Momik well beyond here, because there must be somewhere. This is what his mother said. Yankel remembers: she said it might take a long time to find it; they might have to keep going a long while, he and Momik – even until all this is over. So Yankel thinks now: if they can just keep going long enough, then they will be safe again. Because there has to be a time after this: his mother told him so.

But when he gets to the far side, Yankel comes to a standstill on the mud, and he finds the land before him is sodden and empty. He can see no track, no path that he should follow. Just the lifting darkness, all the distance still to be covered.

Dawn is a cold line at the horizon, and the wind cuts into his face and fingers. Momik cries against his shoulders, crying at the cold: he can't help himself.

Yankel crouches, trying somehow to shield him; to keep him quieter, and to look for the way ahead at the same time. Except he still can't see it. Yankel can't think of his mother's words either, only of his father's face: if his father could see them here.

Then the marsh girl reaches the crest of the road behind him. Yankel hears her; he turns and sees her, relieved at the sight of her – even if he is still so unsure of her.

Her shawl pulled tight against the chill, she leans into the climb, pulling the horse behind her. The animal is unwilling, hesitant about his footing, but he allows himself to be led, clambering awkward but close behind her along the ridge first, and then down the slope too, sending rocks skittering to the muddy ground where Yankel stands up, ready for her to shout, or to rail at him for stealing.

The girl sees him, he knows she does, but she keeps her eyes on the horse, and on where best to find a foothold. Even when she is close enough for talking, the girl says nothing – either about the bundles he took or about Yankel running.

He walks to meet her, holding out the food to her, an apology. Wordless, she takes it from his grasp, and the trailing oilskin from Yankel's arms. The girl already has the other strapped to the horse; she wraps the bundles, lashing them into its folds, and Yankel is grateful to fall in behind her as she pulls the animal onwards.

In this landscape there is only the three of them.

The boy follows her, brother on his back; nothing Yasia can do to stop him. Whenever she turns her head, he is there. So she stops turning.

With the dawn comes rain, and Yasia leads the horse from the track into the undergrowth for shelter. The boy follows her then too, crouching not far from her in the leaf and twig, untying his brother, holding him close.

Drips fall from above, from the mossy curls dangling from the branches, as she waits for the rain to pass over. Yasia has no dry wood for a fire, even if she dared light one; no dry ground to lie on. The smaller one dozes, held in his brother's arms, soft mouth open. Not the older one, though: he is wakeful. Yasia feels how he sits hunched under the blanket he has pulled around them both. Legs drawn up, he shields his young brother from the worst of the wet – and all the time he is watching, searching the chill and dripping scrub around them. He is listening out, Yasia thinks. For the German with the glasses, or just for other Germans. And he expects her to take him somewhere safer. He expects her to know the way.

She pulls the oilskin over her shoulders.

Overtaken by weariness, Yasia sleeps without knowing it, in fits and starts, all through the first chill hours of daylight. Heaving awake again and again, to find that it is still raining, the boys are still there, her fists are still wrapped in the horse's traces.

Until at last the rain stops.

They press on together, for now at least. Through the wet and the cold. The wet meadows. Passing through the waist-deep grasses, growing thick and dank either side of the way they follow; and then on into stands of birch and pine, where the track disappears under root and fallen leaf and needle. Always better to be under cover, Yasia has to steel herself each time they pass out again into open country; her eyes on the next patch of scrub, she keeps on moving.

The older boy carries the small one on his back. She rides ahead of them on the horse, with the bundles strapped across his haunches – and although she rides, the boy keeps pace with her. Each time she thinks he's falling back, he trots to catch up again; it drags on her like a weight, knowing he's there behind her.

But Yasia won't let herself be slowed by him. She only stops if the horse has to drink, filling the pot she took from Osip's at the peaty streams they halt beside. When the older boy catches her up, he crouches, cupping water in his hands, before untying his brother from his shoulders.

Free of his blanket binding, the young one slides down to crouch beside her at the water's edge, and Yasia stands then: she doesn't like them too close. But when the small one fills his palms and drinks, she sees it again: his milk-white and soft brown fineness, even through the dirt streaks on his face and fingers. When she bites into one of the apples from her bundle, he blinks at her, eyes glassy with hunger and from this relentless pressing onwards. So she hands him an apple; Yasia cannot do otherwise. And then another for the older one – even if his face is turned away from her.

But she pushes them onto the horse to eat. Better not to be slowed, she thinks, even now they are over the roadworks.

They barely speak. Most of the time they walk and walk, following where a cart rut, here and there, shows that others have passed through on their way to the marshes, or to the scarce villages on this poor land before them.

Yasia has passed this way before now on her way to her uncle's, and she holds it in her mind all the while as she walks: his small byre, its leaning walls of wooden shingles, the handful of pale cows that filled it. She followed behind that small herd with her mother most autumns, holding the tether, walking the calf born in the spring, which would buy her uncle enough buckwheat to last him through the cold months, if he drove a hard enough bargain.

But his village is surrounded by marshland, and Yasia knows they are entering that wide and empty vastness. She has never led the way through there; she has only ever been led before.

They pass through clearings where the trees are blazed with rough way-markers; Yasia sees leaning shelters made of branches, blackened circles of old cookfires; traces left by traders, or by partisans maybe. But in all their hours and hours of walking they see no one.

And then they have to stop when the light goes.

Yasia leads them into the trees, the thickest she can find

in the dusk. The ground underneath there is soft with fallen leaves; not soft yet like the marshes, but Yasia spreads the oilskin where she feels it is driest.

Still no fire: all she manages is a dark smoulder, striking and striking at the flint while the older one stands and watches. The younger one crouches nearer her, hopeful of flames to warm him, his face blank from the long hours of rocking motion on the horse, on his brother's shoulders.

The animal grazes, the children eat more of the apples, just a little of the meat too; Yasia divides it between them. And then, each rolled in blankets, they pull the sides of the oilskin up to cover them.

Yasia is warm enough, just, to lie down, but not to close her eyes yet. The older boy sits up longer, still sleepless, hollow-eyed with the effort of watching, blinking about himself at the darkening wilderness.

'No Germans will come here,' he ventures, after a while. 'They do not dare,' he says, into the darkness, and then he looks to Yasia, as though for confirmation.

He may just be right. But Yasia can't answer, because she sees, too, that the boy doesn't understand.

She packed food only for one. Only for her, not for three; she never meant to take them. The cart was meant to shelter her, and to carry her; Yasia isn't even sure that she can reach her uncle's without it, not before the food runs out. And if the boys are still with her when she gets there? She hasn't even thought that far. Yasia can think only of the emptiness out here, and the risk to all of them.

She is last to sleep, first to wake. All through those dark hours she thinks how she will leave them; that she must do that, come the morning. But when she leans over the boys at daybreak, she cannot bring herself. Yasia can only shake them.

'We have to keep walking.'

The light rises, the mist drifts, clearing a little before returning; and then, some time late on in the morning, the land grows softer underfoot. Yasia's boots begin sinking into the track they are following – or what passes for a track in this landscape.

It is not long before the older boy sees it too: Yasia hears him calling out on the horse's back, where he sits with his brother. He is pointing behind himself when she turns to look, showing the small one how the hoof prints fill with water, her heel prints too, so they must be getting nearer.

But they are all hungry, all weary, so when they next come to water, she lets the boys slide down from the horse. Yasia tears bread for them to share, and she tells them to sit and eat; the pines here grow thick, and she finds enough dry branches to make a blaze at last. Warmed through, the children doze a little, and Yasia lets them, thinking they will walk faster and further when they have rested.

She bundles up the food again, lashing it to the horse's back, ready to press on as soon as the boys wake, and then Yasia hunkers down near the embers to wait, to feel their warmth against her face. She closes her eyes too, just a short while. Only to sleep with them into the afternoon darkness; Yasia doesn't wake again, bleary, until nightfall.

She scolds herself over the lost hours, building up the fire again. Her empty stomach nags at her, and so does the thought of all those miles they could have put behind them. But the boys blink at her, still weary in the firelight, and the urge to sleep more pulls at her limbs too.

They can go no further until morning, Yasia knows this; and she cannot feed them more if the food is to last them. So she warms water from the stream for them to drink, so their bellies will feel full, even if they aren't. That third night, the small one lies between Yasia and his brother where he will be warmest.

But the night is far colder than the last, and even before dawn they are awake again, the blankets stiff and frost-rimed.

The small one cries then. So there is no more sleeping. They sit and wait for dawn, which comes only slowly, only dimly: the sky low above them and heavy-grey, clouds full of cold rain.

They walk on again as soon as they can see enough. But the young one cries to be carried, he cries to be held; the noise he makes is painful. Even when the older one hoists him onto his shoulders, he doesn't stop his mewling.

Yasia begins to doubt the way then. The noise of the small boy's crying and the wide and wet silence all around them have her confounded.

She thinks: if the track they have picked up again so often wasn't the right one?

There is no sun, just low cloud beyond the branches, and Yasia has lost her bearings. If they have erred off course? They have been erring for hours through these wooded hollows, and still they have seen no village houses. Only sedge and moss, fern and birch, all around them.

They need to get to higher ground; she knows this.

Only the higher ground is possible to farm here, to graze small herds on, as her uncle does. But she also knows the high ground in the marshes is rare, and scarcely different from the low. There are small islands of sloping pasture, but few and far between, and often cut off entirely by the autumn rains; even the forests turn to lakes out here in the cold months, roots submerged, branches dipping into the swampy mire. In amongst the trees as they are, Yasia cannot see far enough to be certain: if their way is clear, or barred already by water.

And if they are lost now?

Yasia says: 'I have to stop.' She wants to think; she has to rest.

But even when they crouch a while by a fallen tree, she can do neither, because the small one will not stop his whimpering, his eyes wet and dark, young brows knitted and clammy, soft mouth puckered with unhappiness.

The older boy holds him; he digs in the younger one's pockets, pulling out his wooden trees, wooden houses, pressing them between his fingers as he murmurs and comforts. But the child will not be distracted by toys or stories.

He will not eat either. So they make him drink, cupping water from the pot, and Yasia feels his cheek, hot against her fingers as she presses him to drink more. His skin is far too hot for a child who is shivering.

She says nothing of this to the older boy. But she sees, too, how limp the small one lies across his lap when he stops his crying, eventually, and sleeps a while, eyes flickering restless under his lids.

The older one whispers to his brother and Yasia watches.

He speaks in his own tongue, and his whispers sound like promises – as feverish as the small one.

His fingers gripped around the wooden forms, his gaze fixed now, the boy looks along the path they were following – but not looking at the same time, his eyes elsewhere. Far beyond the trees somewhere. And Yasia thinks: How far does he think he can keep going?

He holds his brother, falling silent, and Yasia eats a heel of bread, chewing the mouthfuls slowly, her fingers stiff, her lips sore with being too long outside. When the boy sees her picking over the last of the loaf, the last of the meat, he stands up.

'We should keep on now.'

The trees clear a little, even if the sky doesn't clear above them. The clouds are still grey-dark, but the ground slopes here, and the older boy takes them up the low incline, leading the horse on which Yasia is riding. She holds the young one cradled in one arm, gripping the mane with her free hand, heading what she hopes is further north and eastwards.

The ground slopes just enough for her to feel the effort in the horse's tread, swaying behind the older boy's dogged striding; the boy sways too, but he doesn't stop, even now he is tired. They can get further on this ground, Yasia tells herself. At least while they are walking, they still have hope of finding somewhere.

They are trudging this low ridge as the day starts fading, and the ground there is dry, so Yasia says they should stop for the night. The older boy starts rolling out the oilskins even before she has dismounted.

He gathers enough leaf and twig and fallen branches for Yasia to start a small fire, still holding the younger one in her lap, and then he gathers more to feed the flames, once he sees she has set them going. The boy slinks off into the darkness, again and again, returning with armfuls, building a good enough pile to keep the fire stocked until morning.

But the small one is so quiet.

He lies bundled in Yasia's arms, unmoving, with just the white of his face showing, and the dark curls at his hairline plastered to his forehead. So although the fire warms her, still Yasia worries. That they have not found Uncle's village, that they will not find it tomorrow either. They have strayed so far already, what is there to keep them from straying further into nowhere?

Her thoughts are fevered and scattering, they give her no rest, although she sorely needs it. And when she lies down, the ground is rough beneath her hips and shoulders.

Yasia does not wake with the light: the older boy has to wake her.

He bends over her under the dripping branches, shaking her by the shoulder, holding out the horse's traces. His still and sleeping brother clasped to him.

'We have to walk.'

But her mouth is too dry for speaking; Yasia's eyes keep on closing; her head is so leaden with aching weariness, she cannot rise, even when he pulls at her arms.

'We have to find somewhere. We have to. At least find more shelter.'

She tries to answer, but a new ache in her throat won't let her, and Yasia's limbs are folded so strangely under her, she cannot lift herself.

When she opens her eyes again, the boy has brought water.

'I let you sleep,' he says, holding it out to her.

Why can't he let her rest more?

The boy props up her shoulders, and he lets her drink from the pot – cool water.

'But you have to come now,' he says, 'you have to.'

He has folded his too-quiet brother into the oilskin, but the child slides from his arms as he stands: he cannot hold the sleeping weight of him, and Yasia's eyes close again; open and close again.

When next she wakes, he is not there.

The young one is lying beside her, blue-pale and sleeping under the oilskin.

He is too pale, far too still and silent. But Yasia can do nothing for him; her eyes only close again.

In this landscape there is no one.

Yankel rides though the trees, all the while the girl and Momik are sleeping. First in one direction, then another, ducking under branches, sinking into hollows, seeking signs of people. He cuts notches into trunks, slashing at the bark with his clasp knife, peeling away its darkness to reveal the pale wood, so he will have a path to return by.

But each time he returns to the girl and his sleeping brother, more hours have passed, and still he has found no help. None for Momik, nobody to help the girl either.

Yankel rides further. Out into the wide and wet silence. He crosses streams, striking out towards the horizon. Still cutting his marks, peeling back the bark, but putting far more distance than he wants to between himself and Momik.

He cannot say how many hours he does this. Hunger comes and passes, thirst too; only the cold stays, only the fear increases. Yankel is frightened of losing his brother, of leaving him too far behind himself. But he also fears stopping, and the coming winter darkness.

His thoughts turn in circles: if he cannot find someone, if he cannot find somewhere, the dark might take him, or it might take Momik. This idea is so appalling it keeps returning, along with a new and worse thought: that he will have to go on without him. That this may be the only way left open.

When the day begins fading, Yankel finds himself among birches, in amongst their pale trunks, uncertain of his bearings; unable to find his notches. The horse slows and he does not know which way to drive it onwards, only that the animal's coat is streaked with damp, and its head hangs low to the ground. Yankel thinks of the failing light, and how he must go on searching; even now, when he doesn't know which way to turn. But his fingers are cold and curled into the coarse mane, and he has been looking for so long, he doesn't trust his senses when it comes:

The smell of stove-wood burning and something cooking over it.

Smoke from a chimney; a thin column rising above the far trees. And then people, finally, the first he has seen in days.

Yankel slides from the horse's back, crashing through the fallen leaves; and there, just ahead of him, is a couple: bent under baskets of stove-wood, and slowing to stare at him.

'Come, please!'

Stooped with concern, they crouch over the girl. The man tugs the shawl back from her forehead, and her plaits are dark with sweat and damp, wide cheeks pale against the leafy ground.

It took so long to get them to follow him, it took so long to find Momik and the girl again, and now Yankel can't understand what they say to one another. They speak in hurried whispers, but he hopes they see the girl's marsh features; that they will take her in now and help her – and Momik too – because the light is failing. He lifts his brother, thinking how close he came to leaving him. Yankel holds him, thinking if he and Momik can sleep now, if they can just eat something and sleep a day or two in the warmth somewhere. But when Yankel steps forward to ask, the couple are already lifting the girl between them.

They leave their stove-wood bundles, hoisting her onto the horse's back, lying her along his neck, and then the woman holds her there while the man leads the animal. Yankel has to follow them, bent under the weight of his brother, under the weight of all the days spent walking. Do they mean to go without him?

They don't take him the way they came, pressing ahead, leading the horse on and on through the darkening branches. Yankel sees no cart ruts, no track they might be following; they say nothing of where they are taking the girl.

Faltering among the tree roots, he loses sight of them: Yankel has to look where he is treading; he has to look ahead too, to keep track of them, if he is not to be alone out here when night comes. He hoists Momik higher, but even then he can't go fast enough to catch them up, and he can't stop to tie Momik to his back for fear of losing them entirely.

Yankel cries out. But they don't hear him. They start to call out themselves now, but Yankel can't see why or who they call to. He can only blunder behind them, following the noise they make.

The couple have taken the girl to a clearing, crossing it far ahead of him; when Yankel gets out from among the trees he catches sight of them under the last of the evening light – and that it is a small hut they head for, half hidden in the branches on the far side. The couple call out, again and again, even before they get to it, their shrill noise carrying, alarming across the clearing, driving Yankel into a run now.

Roused by their cries, a woman comes from the doorway; she rushes at them through the falling dusk. Yankel sees how she pulls the girl's shawl back from her face too – and that as soon as the woman sees her, she points them onwards.

A clanging sounds out, metal on metal, as Yankel ducks into the trees again after them. He glances over his shoulder: it is the woman sounding out a call, like a warning, ladle against a pot lid, and then bit by bit, her ringing is answered by another, and another, further ahead, beyond the darkening trunks.

Momik slips in his arms; Yankel can't carry his brother much further, his hands and shoulders cramped and aching. But he can follow the sound, even when the couple pass out of sight again between the branches. And the ringing does not stop, even as the path rises; it rises and turns again as they pass out from the trees and into meadowland.

Low enclosures are dotted here; Yankel sees a new one each time he lifts his head to look. They come first to one house and then another – always more of them – and then villagers begin emerging from the low doors as they pass. Farmers, cautious and frowning; mothers holding their children. Some follow with their eyes, others follow behind them, this halting procession; Yankel feels them catching him up, and then he sees them overtaking, his arms sore and weakening, his legs folding under him. The villagers turn to look at him, and then they turn away again, leaving him and Momik behind themselves.

The ringing dies away as they come to the far meadows, nearing the edge of the settlement, and the quiet leaves Yankel all the more uncertain. All the trees here are bare, the trunks are black and wet, and now a sleety rain is falling. It chills his face and his fingers, shrouding the path from view, the girl and the couple too, even the villagers who follow them.

Until there, up in the pasture, is an old man.

His head bent low against the weather, Yankel sees he is bringing in his cows, walking stiff beside the oldest of his animals, dun and wide-hipped, mother to the others. Clicking and whistling, he keeps the small herd moving, their legs muddied up to their udders, almost, their hooves sinking in the soft ground; and when he lifts his face, the girl raises a hand to him.

She is pulled from the horse by many village arms, and the

old man stands where he is, his cows stand with him in the sleet, watching the girl as she is carried towards him through the long grass, already yellowed with the cold. Stubble grows thick and white, feathery under his chin, and his face is lined and creased, but his cheekbones are wide, his eyes set deep in their sockets, just like the girl's, and they uncloud as he takes her in.

'Yasia?'

There is a welcome there, Yankel sees it as he approaches, how the man puts out both his hands to her. But there is confusion as well, his old eyes blinking, disconcerted: he sees how weak she is, the girl's legs barely holding her as she is lowered to stand before him. Who comes to the marshes at such a time, and in such a way? It can only mean bad news. The old man's gaze shifts to Yankel and to Momik, too; these brothers who are not her brothers, and who have come to a stop behind her.

'They are yours also?' one of the villagers asks, and the old man looks at them, doubtful.

The girl turns to look at Yankel. Eyes fevered in confusion, as though she can't remember any longer. How they got here. How she got here with them.

The villagers' eyes are on him, and Yankel wills them all to see it: how Momik sleeps too quietly, he must be taken care of. He has carried him this far, and as soon as Momik is strong again, he will carry him further. Surely they must see that.

9

The snows are deep that winter, and they hold for weeks. The sodden landscape freezing over, turning grey-white and still, as far as the horizon.

Yasia saw it as soon as she was well enough to sit up and look out through the window: how the small scattering of houses was held by drifts as high as the eaves, closed in by the cold. It was a relief to be closed off.

'My sister's daughter.'

Uncle pointed at Yasia when his neighbours called for their milk those first mornings. He was careful to point her out to all those who had not seen their arrival, who had only heard it, or heard about it.

The villagers stamped the mud and slush from their boots, stepping over the threshold. They stood and stared at Yasia, wrapped in blankets at one end of his long and single room, and then at the two boys.

'From my sister's district.' Yasia's uncle nodded tersely in the boys' direction.

This was just about all Yasia heard him say about them, and it was not a lie: that was not his way. Yasia saw his marsh pride would not allow him to lie to his neighbours.

'It is safer they stay here. For the meantime,' Uncle told them, gesturing at the children first, weak with fever, and then at the sleet that was turning to snow and settling on everything.

The snow kept on falling, and it seemed reason enough for them to stay here. It seemed to put off his neighbours' questions, too, because the villagers kept on coming. Yasia saw them, as if through a veil; how they let Uncle fill their pails and jugs, as always, carrying their milk off along the village paths. And so the news spread, and her uncle's word was accepted, for the meanwhile in any case, because soon no one stared any longer.

Far from everything, Yasia slept and slept, even after the fever left her. Even after the two boys were well enough to stand and walk again, her legs were still weak, arms too heavy to lift. Any light made her eyes ache: the morning sun on the snow outside, and the lamps Uncle lit in the afternoons.

He brought her soup in a bowl from the stove, sitting her up to drink it; drawing up a stool to sit with her until she'd finished.

'You must eat now.'

Uncle did the same for the boys, in his bachelor way. He was unused to children, but Yasia saw his rough care for them, especially the younger one. The first to get well again, the boy climbed out from the blankets long before his brother could; standing and shivering while Uncle set a blaze in the stove each morning. Uncle found him an over-shirt from another village child, cutting it down to size, pulling it over his head so the boy would be warmer; and he tried to glean the small one's name from his timid murmurings, guessing at *Marek* and *Maksim* and *Mirko*. His brother was still too ill to confirm which, so Uncle took to calling the small boy any one of these, because he lifted his head to all of them, his eyes following Uncle around the room, shy at his gruffness, and curious. As soon as he got strong enough to stand, he followed Uncle outside, standing at the threshold in his stockinged feet to watch him cross the yard.

Uncle cut strips of leather to replace the boy's broken laces, binding his soles in hide strips, so the snow and cold wouldn't get in through the holes. He did the same for the older one, too – both the boys' good shoes had been walked half to ruins on the way here.

But Uncle also went outside alone sometimes, to meet with his neighbours: Yasia saw him, standing out beyond the byre, on the snow-covered track there. At the meeting of the ways, where all the village men gathered whenever there were village matters to discuss. Such a group they made, and such a long time they talked there, despite the cold. Just far enough from the house that she couldn't hear them; their backs turned, as though they didn't want her eyes on them either.

As soon as she was stronger, Yasia was careful to make herself useful.

—

Rising in the quiet before dawn, in the deep quiet of the snows, she pulls on her skirts and her apron in the half dark, pulling at the older one's elbow, putting out his shoes where he will easily find them.

Now she is well again, they share one bed, one bracken-stuffed mattress on the floor between the three of them, sleeping together behind the curtaining blanket Uncle tacked across the ceiling when they first came. Uncle's own bed is on the other side of the long room, closer to the stove, where he pulls it each winter now he is older, and they are careful not to wake him, or the younger one; they leave them slumbering.

The older boy walks beside Yasia to the byre as day is breaking. Still sleep-dulled, both of them, they don't speak any more than they need to, but Yasia sees how well the boy attends to his tasks, clearing the stalls, forking the hay into the mangers. He has never offered his name, even when Yasia has asked for it; the boy has still never offered her more than a word or two, and there is no talking to someone who is silent. But all the while she is milking, he lifts the full pails without once being told, emptying them into the churns before carefully returning them.

Uncle taught him to do all this while Yasia could do nothing but sleep. By the time she was well enough to work again, the boy could milk cows – the docile ones anyway – skim the cream, and sharpen the axes her uncle uses for firewood. So this is what he does now every morning, working alongside her in the stalls first, and then on the whetstone. Yasia sees his industry, and his satisfaction: the way he sharpens until the axe blades can slice a cornstalk from the straw bales, while she sweeps and kneels and scrubs the pails. She presses her cheek into the cows' warm flanks as she milks them, looking out into the darkness lifting beyond the doorway of the byre, gazing at the icicles that have grown all winter, all along the lintel there, as the boy works on behind her. And over the weeks that this continues, Yasia gets accustomed to the quiet between them.

Uncle comes after sun-up, stiff and slow along the frozen path they have trodden through the snow from the house to the cows, and when he steps in through the doorway, the older boy stands up to receive the day's instructions.

Uncle calls him 'you there' and 'boy', but the child shows no sign of wanting it any other way. He splits firewood now like he was born to it, making sure there is stove-wood stacked high and dry under the lean-to, and kindling in the basket. Uncle takes him to the forest, too, with the other menfolk, when more logs need to be felled and fetched to heat the houses, or make repairs. And when it turns out that wood is what the boy does best, Uncle takes him from one village house to the next, all through the winter dark and the frost, teaching the boy to shape the shingles while he makes good the neighbours' walls.

The boy has to be taught all this: he is no farmer's son; Yasia thinks her uncle will have understood as much. But if any more words have passed between them, she doesn't know. She isn't sure she wants to, either. Yasia only hopes her uncle sees that the boy is as useful as she is – more so.

When she watches him carry Uncle's axe at his side, shouldering timber, Yasia thinks how he carried his brother all the way here; he kept on going, even when she had to stop. The boy is the one who got her here through the marshes.

But when he is in the house now, his eyes are always elsewhere, turned outside, on the snowdrifts and the bare trees, as though he looks beyond them. As if he would be gone from here, if he could only brave the cold; if only he could carry his brother through it.

In the afternoons, when the light goes, his brother takes out the wooden houses, and the small trees he carved for him. The child arranges them across the mattress in the lamplight, playing and murmuring stories; he lifts one to look at it closely, or sometimes to show Yasia. But she never sees the older one touch them any longer.

He sits at the window, his eyes on the horizon, even after the dark comes, and then she wonders: if he will be gone one morning when she wakes up. If he would leave his brother here, even; strike out alone for somewhere beyond the marshes. Yasia doesn't know what he looks for out there, but she tries to read his features.

Twice, Uncle takes the older one to meet with the elders, out in the snow, at the meeting of the tracks.

He leaves the boy standing to one side, while he steps among the menfolk, and it is clear from their glances, sidelong and cautious, that he and his brother are discussed there. It is clear from his closed face that the boy doesn't like it.

But Yasia cannot tell if anything is decided; how long they can stay here. She doesn't know who has the say here.

—

The small one is left to her in the meantime. Yasia has the weight of him leaning against her at the stove-side, the tug of his small fists at her skirts as she kneads and sews. When Uncle is home, the small one watches him intently; when his brother is there, it is his brother he still prefers – but Yasia has his fineness to herself in the daytime hours.

On days when the women and children go to gather kindling, he walks beside her out to the forests, running ahead of her where the trees grow thickest, and there is little snow underfoot to slow him. His cheeks redden as he grows stronger, and she sees his first smiles too, as he bends and gathers with the other village children, squatting with Yasia and the village mothers while she binds his small armfuls of twigs and branches into bundles. The women sing the village songs while they work, and the boy hums the same tunes as Yasia carries him home again on her shoulders, his cheek resting sleepy against her shawled head.

The village men they pass nod to her, and they nod to the boy in silent acknowledgement; all the village knows him.

They know the older boy too. His quiet ways, his closed face. But Yasia sees him sometimes in the afternoons, returning from the forest at the same time as they do, and how he never gives more than a half-nod to anyone in passing; to her either.

Yasia wishes he would give more than that.

Because for all that he works hard in the daytime, at night, in the dark behind their curtain, he often lies wakeful: she feels him, from where she lies on the other side of the small one.

Yasia doesn't dare guess at what he thinks of then. What he remembers.

Thoughts come at her, too – regardless – of Myko and of soldiers – too raw to speak out loud. Yasia feels they seek her out, in the watches of the night, and they leave her too sore for sleeping. She knows how it hurts to think back, and how hard it is not to.

Here, at least, there is no one to run from. Only the partisans.

The women beat their pot lids in warning, as soon as one of the fighters is sighted coming in from the forests. Yasia has come to know this sound, always followed by the slam of doors and shutters, while the mothers hide their children, and the men lie still in the byres and the feed bins.

The fighters come demanding: food and clothes and blankets. They come late one afternoon, when the sun is already red and setting, and they fire their rifles in the air, at the meeting of the tracks. Yasia sees them in the well-trodden snow there; she keeps watch on them through the gaps in the shingles, crouched in the dark space behind the manger, where they all crawl to hide themselves.

Uncle sits hunched beside her, beside the brothers, while the men stand outside with their rifles, waiting and waiting.

'They will wait until dark, and even after,' he mutters. 'Until we give them what they came for.'

The fighters want meat and meal to last them, boots to get them through the winter, and Uncle tells Yasia he gave at first.

'Much too much,' he says. 'Better never to have given. Perhaps, perhaps.'

He calls the fighters bandits, and says there are so many different packs of them.

'This village is theirs. They've laid claim to us. They say they will protect us from raiders, as well as from the Germans. So they will always come for payment,' Uncle whispers, bitter. 'And what can we do?'

The drifts around the fighters are deep, blue-cold in the last of the day's light, and the men have a wild look about them. Their boots wrapped in rags, bodies draped in felt and fur and sacking, in stolen German greatcoats and torn Red Army tunics; they make Yasia uneasy. She sees how the older boy watches them, intent, blinking in the shafts of cold light between the shingles; the same look on his face as when he turns his eyes to the horizon.

Uncle sees him watching too. He tells Yasia: 'Boys have gone to those outlaws, from other marsh villages,' lifting his chin at the oldest brother, as if he thinks this one might get the same idea. Then he squints out at the fighters himself.

'This pack would bring the war back through here, if they could. But just to bring the Russians back. You understand?' Uncle pokes the older boy, to be sure that he hears this. But the boy gives no sign – his eyes only on the fighters.

'You see those guns they wave? Do you?' Uncle persists, and the boy shrugs; he gives one of his half nods, and Uncle sucks his teeth, impatient.

'Those are Russian rifles,' Uncle tells him. 'They were found in the thickets where the Red soldiers threw them when they ran away from the Germans. Are you listening to me?'

The boy turns to him, reluctant.

'Haven't you had enough?' Uncle asks. 'There'll be more

war, more Germans, everywhere beyond the marshes, as soon as the snows are gone.'

Uncle falls silent. But not like he's finished talking, just taking his time, regarding the boy, his small brother beside him.

And then:

'One more thing,' he says. 'They wouldn't have you. None of the bandits would. Don't think for a moment they'd take someone of your kind.'

The boy's face tightens; Yasia's chest also.

Uncle knows. He must have known all along that the brothers are Jew boys, and Yasia could curse herself for hoping otherwise. But she can't think now, only that the boys are not safe here; and then the old man points out at the fighters.

'They all want the Germans gone, just like you do. But don't be thinking that makes you welcome.'

He waits then, as if for an answer, a response of some sort: Yasia thinks her Uncle wants something more than the usual half nod from this boy now. But the boy does nothing save to blink at him, eyes bright and hard with tears that he won't allow himself. He blinks them away and then he turns to look outside again.

Uncle sucks his teeth. He would shout, Yasia can see that, but for the fighters, who would come and chase them from their hiding place; they would chase all the food from the larder. And what would they do to these brothers?

Yasia pulls the small one into her lap, because if Uncle knows about the boys, then so must the elders; so must every one of the villagers. What will they say once the snows have gone?

She peers again through the gaps in the shingles.

A woman is hurrying through the drifts towards the fighters. At first Yasia is frightened: that the woman will turn and point, just like the timber man's wife, back in Osip's yard; that she will tell the bandits about the Jew boys in the cow byre.

But the woman's arms are too full for that. Yasia sees the loaves in the crook of her elbow, and the neck of a bottle, too, that the men make a grab for, lifting it to the evening light. Probably that's what the men want most, she tells herself: something warming. It eases her fears a little to think so, and it makes the fighters seem less like strangers. Her father always took a bottle with him if he had to work out in the snows; Myko's grandfather too.

But then she thinks of Mykola.

Yasia holds the small one closer.

They crawl to their beds after the fighters are gone again, and she lies a long while in the dark there, thinking too much for sleep to come.

When the snows are gone. Yasia doesn't like to think of it. Of her uncle being right, and the Germans taking everywhere beyond the marshes. Or of all that may have to be given up, if they are to live to see them gone again.

Is it better to strike out alone for the horizon? Or better to run and hide as they do, than to fire a Russian rifle, than to wear a German greatcoat? Yasia thinks of Myko in his armband. *Better to run.* Better he had deserted; better that than do another's bidding, surely.

But those thoughts are still so raw, and thoughts of who

or what to fight for too confusing. Yasia turns to the quiet forms beside her.

'Better to hide,' she whispers to the small one who lies warm at her side, although he sleeps too soundly to heed her.

'Better to lie low,' she continues, because she knows the almost-grown one is lying sleepless just beyond him, and she wants him to hear her.

'Best to sit it out.'

Though who can say how long they'll be allowed to sit it out here?

Epilogue

Ukraine, early 1942

Arnold is already driving at sun-up, along the frost-grey country tracks, as the first light rises on a clear and new year's morning.

Snow is still banked either side of the cart road, and the surface is rutted, but it has frozen overnight so it is passable, and his driver steers the jeep at pace, skirting the potholes, passing fields and farmsteads, all frost-rimed and empty.

It is still too early for farmhands to be working. The Sturmbannführer knows that soon they will be out, to break the ice in the drinking troughs, fork the hay for the animals, but for now it is just the first lamps he sees burning in the farm kitchens. He glimpses their yellow flicker, here and there across the field and pasture beyond the breath-fogged windscreen, and even once beyond the branches, in the darkness of a small woodland he passes into.

His driver has to slow there: the track is softer, and the trees grow dense beside it, and the man has to wind down his window and check that the tyres are not sinking too far into the mire. Arnold shifts, uncomfortable at the smell of mud and leaf mould rising. He is uncertain, too, of the gloom around him – and of the lamplight among the trees there. The marshes are still full of bandits. Despite his frequent warnings, his superiors have not yet sent reinforcements, and Arnold feels himself watched from beyond the windscreen.

But then the wheels find their grip again and the jeep lurches forward, and the track turns eastward, too. So when they emerge from the forest, finally, Arnold finds they are driving into the sunrise.

The damp on the windscreen catches the sunlight, and the driver has to slow the jeep again, shielding his eyes with his forearm, but Arnold sits up straighter, peering intrigued through the smears as he rubs the glass clear again. Because even through their blur, he can see the new road in front of him.

Still distant, but it is unmistakable: a high and straight line under the horizon.

It cuts across the fields and ditches and over the streams that still lie frozen; over all the hedge-and-post peasant markers of the land boundaries – clean across the territory before him.

The sight of it gives him pause first, and then it has him hurrying his driver: 'There, man. Faster. You can see where we are now.'

It is the final stretch to be completed. Arnold has had to

come out almost daily these past weeks to all the different stretches, the different encampments, to inspect the surfacing: that it has really been finished to standard, as all the foremen have reported.

These duties have fallen to Arnold since Pohl's arrest. He has been supervising schedules, the delivery of materials, the quality and speed of work, as well as seeing to all the usual commitments of his Sturmbannführer's life here. At times, it has weighed on him like a burden. Left him wondering if he was capable; in the eyes of his superiors and of his peers (Arnold has heard the whispers), even in his own estimation.

But today Arnold rose early. He sent for the driver even before first light, deliberately, to ensure he'd be alone out here. Without anyone looking over his shoulder, or passing comment, without the banality of small talk, too – he is amazed at the number of his colleagues who can talk only of small things, even as they undertake this largest of all enterprises. Arnold has sought out solitude, some driving and thinking time – and now he has come upon the road sooner than expected.

What he sees is a long embankment, like a rampart; like the earthworks of ancient times, but new and clean somehow. A proud and stately causeway, new-laid across the terrain here.

Lifted by this unexpected sight, Arnold unbuckles the jeep roof, folding it back, the better to contemplate it; and then, once the driver has parked, he leaves the vehicle, telling his man to wait by the drainage ditch, climbing the low slope alone.

Stepping onto the tarmac, coming to a standstill, Arnold feels it underfoot now, not just weighing on his shoulders:

this road he has had to take on, and that has threatened to take over everything these past months.

But it makes an impressive sight this morning. The sheer length of it completed, for one thing – but it is more than that. Wide and dark and even, the surface is just touched with frost, and with light from the rising day, and it stretches ever onwards, both before and behind him. The slopes that buttress it fall away steeply to either side, into the rough country where a cold mist still lingers – but the road is lifted, it seems. Above the damp and mist, and above the plain, still dotted with snow-mounds and hollows; above everything, or so it seems to Arnold. Even the far stands of birches and the woodland he passed through seem low by comparison.

The road hovers as though suspended, cutting a swathe across these wet lands; visible for miles around, it must be. And it stretches ever onwards, as though unending, meeting the rise of the land – perhaps even the curve of the earth – and then cresting it, into the rose-and-blue distance.

It pleases him to see it like this. And Arnold knows it is not just the sunrise colouring everything this morning: it is the road itself that brings such satisfaction. The slow and even rise of it, the solidity of it underfoot; the fine grade of tarmac, resistant to water ingress; the gentle curve of the camber. Arnold looks at the road, clear and sound and durable, running wide and smooth away from him in either direction, and he thinks that he did well to listen to Pohl – about engineering matters, in any case.

It even feels like his road just then; his own achievement; this stretch of it, at least. Arnold thinks he fought for it, after all: even while Pohl was still here and doing his job, he had to argue with his superiors – over the sheer number of labourers required, of course, but above all over the cost of these materials. Arnold could not have used lesser ones – not once Pohl had explained things: how fine a road they could build here. And now Arnold gazes at the result a good few minutes, gratified by the sight.

What would Pohl say?

It is impossible not to ask himself. This road was the engineer's, before it was his, Arnold concedes. It was made to last; made to his specifications. The man insisted he build this road well enough to last a human lifespan, and even beyond that. *Is this Reich not meant to outlast all of us small mortals?*

Arnold has not followed Pohl's case since he left the district.

He made his report on the man's conduct – he had to – but he'd wanted no part in it beyond that. He can imagine what ensued, though, and Arnold imagines it again as he stands there. The knock on the door in the small hours; the bare and brutal little room for Pohl to end his days in. Soon there will be the coldly official letter for his wife to open: *died whilst trying to escape; died at his own hand*, or some other such bleak Gestapo fiction.

The man should have listened to him. *If Pohl had listened*, Arnold tells himself, frowning as he remembers.

His breath comes in clouds, and he is a little stiff this morning, his legs and shoulders. He's been like this all these past weeks since the round-up, since the Jews were dealt with: bent out of shape by all he's seen through. By the demands of this damned posting.

But here he is still.

And here too is this strange lightness; this good road and this gratitude for it – so unexpected.

Arnold blinks at the wide-open country around him, and then he reminds himself that it does not help to think of Pohl, or of all the darkness he has encountered here. Only that he has this lightness this morning, and how much this is worth.

He decides to leave the car and walk, in order to savour it this morning. Who is there to stop him? He can follow this stretch of road on foot, take his time and enjoy it – he can even walk to the next encampment. Arnold is due at the far-eastern one at midday, but the one to the west is just two kilometres, three kilometres away: a good stretch for walking, and a thorough distance to be checking for surface quality. So if anyone should ask what he was doing, he will tell them: *Admiring the good road I had built here.* It occurs to him that if he walks westwards, he will in some way – even if in just a small way – be walking homewards. So, as this is the thought Arnold prefers, he turns now, thankful to feel the winter sun at his shoulders.

He buttons his tunic against the cold, pulling his greatcoat around himself. But Arnold doesn't start walking, not quite yet, because his eyes are caught by something on the horizon. Is there movement there?

He cocks his head, unsure what he is hearing, if he is hearing something at all, and at first there is only quiet, the frost-held stillness. But then it comes again, just as he sets off walking: a distant thrum in the cold air, like a pulsing. And although Arnold keeps on striding, the thrum keeps on getting louder; it soon becomes a drone, loud enough to slow him.

Arnold halts on the road then, under the cold and clear sunrise, and he waits and watches the far line where the sky meets the flatlands. Because the noise is accompanied by a darkness, a mass advancing; he can see it now. It is still distant – still indistinct – but gaining ground and volume; and along with the drone, shapes are forming there, and growing.

Trucks: Arnold can make them out. Field-grey vehicles: it is a military convoy. *Wehrmacht* and darker: Arnold sees an army unit with *Waffen* SS behind it.

Troops are coming through the district.

But these are earlier than he had expected.

Midday, he was told: Arnold is to be at the eastern encampment to see the convoys passing, along with all his brother officers. So perhaps this is merely an advance guard – but the troops he sees are impressive nonetheless.

The battalion on the horizon is gaining form and substance as it draws closer, and Arnold is glad to have caught this: he is seeing this convoy ahead of all the other SS in the district.

Most of it is artillery, judging by the vehicles; judging by the noise they are making. Trucks are first and behind them come vans, then tanks. And behind them? There must be armaments; Arnold imagines machine guns and field guns and mortars, all mounted in rows on the backs of lorries.

He has long waited for this: to see the Reich make use of this road for its armies. For taking Odessa and Kharkov, Crimea, Sebastopol; clawing out more of that oil and grain land; claiming more workers for the Reich factories – perhaps even for clearing the marshes here of bandits, finally, as he's so often requested.

Arnold is aware, too, that there is another road being laid to the north of here – on the far side of the marshes; parallel, almost, to the road he stands on – and the mass of troops is so clear now, drawing ever nearer, so he wonders as he watches, if that other road has been completed. If there is another convoy tearing along there, even now, roaring on to claim Moscow and the continent beyond it.

For a moment, Arnold feels the grandeur of the Reich's expansion; its enormity, set against his own human smallness.

But then he falters.

Because they will not stop, these soldiers: no reason for them to slow or stop on this road, built wide enough and well enough to hold them, so Arnold backs away now.

Turning for the car again, he steps off the tarmac onto the rubble sloping, a little too hastily. Arnold misses his footing, just briefly, but just long enough to throw him, and to have him glancing over his shoulder at the road and the advancing forces.

And then he finds himself thinking, as he stumbles, of the man who gave so much to build it for them.

The first warm dawns bring a trickling along the shingles. A dripping from the icicles. Yasia watches the bright drops falling from the lintel in the mornings, face pressed to the belly of the cow she is milking.

Not long after, walking back from the byre, she sees the dark of earth and grass again in her melting footprints.

The snow still sits packed in drifts at the house-sides; Yasia finds it heaped against the tallest trunks at the edge of the woodland when she is out with the youngest and gathering kindling. But it drops, abruptly, from the branches. It slides from the roofs too, sudden and wet, from the houses in the cleft of land below the forest. The rush of the tumbling snow makes the young one start and gasp, and seek out the safety of Yasia's skirts. They stand among the trunks, hand in hand, watching as it slips first from one village house and then the next.

Soon the snow clears wherever the sun reaches. The ground gives again underfoot, wherever it is trodden.

All is sink and softness, drip and gurgle. And this fills Yasia with misgivings.

People pass again through the village. She sees other marsh dwellers, on their way to other villages: more each day, it seems. Some stop to sell, some stop to buy, calling for milk and curds at Uncle's byre.

They stop and talk at all the village houses, passing on all the winter's births and deaths, the season's arguments and truces. Word spreads fast from mouth to mouth across the marshes of all the winter's departures and arrivals.

Once the snow melts, word can be sent to her mother that she is safe, Yasia knows this. But word spreading about the boys makes her frightened, because all is still to be discussed and decided.

It is enough to make Yasia stop the boys from going outside.

As soon as the tracks are clear enough, the priest comes to the village, pulled in an ox cart, stiff and upright, his robes on under his travelling blankets. Yasia sees his arrival as he passes the windows; it has her standing, sudden and shocked, spilling the small boy's milk across the table.

The elder is there to receive him at the meeting of the tracks. Yasia watches their solemn handshake, she hears their salutation – and then how her uncle is called out to join them, his boots already tied, as if he has been waiting for this.

The three men stand with their heads bent together in earnest talking; it is a back and forth – between the priest and Uncle first, and then the priest and the elder – and Yasia thinks that now it is all over; the elder has heard all he needs and has reached his verdict. The boys will be sent off, not welcome here either.

But then Uncle calls to her to take off her apron.

'Dress the boys, child. Bring the brothers with you.'

In the end, it comes unasked. In the reeds, by the still-frozen riverside the following morning.

Out on the ice, Uncle bends tentative with his axe, chipping and chipping at the thaw, while Yasia stands with the two boys at the shoreline, in amongst the small throng gathered there.

Whole families have turned out, the first time so many from the marshlands have gathered together since the snows came; the old cocooned in blankets, the youngest wrapped tight in swaddling clothes. The sons are scrubbed, all the young daughters' hair is plaited, elaborate around their temples; and Yasia stands upright among them, hands clasped with the two brothers either side of her.

The young one watches everything, dark eyes alert as the

people sing and murmur; the older one's face is harder to read, although Yasia tries as the priest calls for quiet.

Then Uncle's boots scuff the frozen surface around the dark hole he has opened. He dips the pail and lifts out the waters, and they are passed hand to hand until they reach the shoreline.

The priest blesses them and raises them to the morning light, and then they are poured, cold and clear, on the brothers' foreheads.

The young one turns to Yasia first, in puzzlement, and then he lifts his face to the skies, and he laughs out loud in his surprise.

The villagers turn to him; nodding to Yasia, they return his smiles, some even his laughter. And all the while the priest keeps on his blessing, pouring the water on the handful of village children born under Stalin, and on the newest village baby, born in the frosts, held tight now in her mother's arms. Yasia watches to one side, the low spring morning light in her eyes as she takes it all in: the baby's cries, the priest's wide palms and his murmured intoning; the older one's solemn face, just as wet as his younger brother's smiling one.

The sunlight plays on the water, sun and shadow passing across the older boy's features, and it is as hard to know what he is thinking.

But then, back at the elder's house, the boys' birth dates and names are scratched into the priest's ledger, and onto the sheaves of village papers; and on the bench outside the window, they sit close beside one another, Yasia and the older one. The small one lies across them, half on her lap, half on his, and it is almost warm then, with the sun on their faces and their backs against the stone wall. Each with their own thoughts, no need for talking. Of all that is no longer. Or can't be made right again. Of times to come, that can't be guessed at yet.

In this quiet meanwhile, in the room behind them, sand is scattered on the ink to dry it, and then all the men present shake hands on their agreement: the older one is Yevhen, and the young one is Mirek; Yasia will teach him until it falls from his tongue.

So, if anyone should come asking, the two of them are marsh boys.

Acknowledgements

My thanks to Dr Beate Meyer at the Institut für die Geschichte der Deutschen Juden in Hamburg, who pointed me in the direction of this story when I was writing another entirely; and to Dr Beate Kosmala at the Zentrum für Antisemitismusforschung in Berlin, whose essay on Willi Ahrem, a Haupttruppführer in the Organisation Todt, inspired this book.

Ahrem's experiences inspired Otto Pohl's, but Pohl is a character of my own invention; any personal similarity with Ahrem, or any other person of the time, is unintentional.

I am indebted to many other historians and scholars whose work has informed my own. Key among them, for this novel, have been Karel Berkhoff and Wendy Lower.

Artem Koslov kindly provided the translations of the Ukrainian dialogue; he and his family also advised on names for my Ukrainian characters.

Any errors in this novel are my own.

I am grateful to my agents Toby Eady and Veronique Baxter for unstinting support, and to all at the David Higham Agency. To my editors: Lennie Goodings for her impeccable judgement, and Dan Frank for always setting the bar high. To the staff at Goldsmiths Library, the British Library and the Imperial War Museum photo archive.

Thank-you to Carl Holland for listening while I thought out loud. To Courttia Newland for strengthening my resolve. To Matt Griffiths for asking (see? I did it). And above all to Michael.

virago

To buy any of our books and to find out more
about Virago Press and Virago Modern Classics,
our authors and titles, as well as events and
book club forum, visit our websites

www.virago.co.uk
www.littlebrown.co.uk

and follow us on Twitter

@ViragoBooks

To order any Virago titles p & p free in the UK,
please contact our mail order supplier on:

+ 44 (0)1832 737525

Customers not based in the UK should contact
the same number for appropriate postage
and packing costs.